MURDER AT THE GALLERY

A Northwest Cozy Mystery - Book 6

BY

DIANNE HARMAN

Copyright © 2018 Dianne Harman

All rights reserved, including the right to reproduce this book, or portions thereof, in any form without written permission except for the use of brief quotations embodied in critical articles and reviews.

Published by: Dianne Harman
www.dianneharman.com

Interior, cover design and website by
Vivek Rajan

This is a work of fiction. Names, characters, places, and incidents either are the product of the author's imagination or are used fictitiously, and any resemblance to actual persons, living or dead, business establishments, events, or locales, is entirely coincidental.

ISBN: 978-1985300453

CONTENTS

Acknowledgments

Prologue

1	Chapter One	1
2	Chapter Two	7
3	Chapter Three	15
4	Chapter Four	24
5	Chapter Five	30
6	Chapter Six	38
7	Chapter Seven	45
8	Chapter Eight	51
9	Chapter Nine	57
10	Chapter Ten	65
11	Chapter Eleven	71
12	Chapter Twelve	77
13	Chapter Thirteen	85
14	Chapter Fourteen	90
15	Chapter Fifteen	96
16	Chapter Sixteen	101
17	Chapter Seventeen	114
18	Chapter Eighteen	121

19	Epilogue	126
20	Recipes	129
21	About Dianne	136
22	Surprise!	138

ACKNOWLEDGMENTS

A few months ago, my husband and I were in an art gallery in Laguna Beach, California, that specializes in California Plein Air Art, a movement that became popular in the early 20th century. Paintings in this genre were created primarily by artists who painted outdoors, thus the name. We collect and enjoy this type of art. The owner of the gallery, Ray Redfern, who is an extremely knowledgeable art dealer, was talking to us about unscrupulous people who try to pass off fake paintings as originals. The seed for the book you are about to read, Murder at the Gallery, came from that conversation.

My thanks to Ray for answering my numerous questions about how something like producing and selling a fake painting could be accomplished. I knew this practice existed, but I didn't know how it was done. Now I do.

If you appreciate fine art or if you find yourself in the Laguna Beach area, you'll not do better than to visit Redfern Gallery, 1540 South Coast Highway, Laguna Beach. Ask for Ray and tell him I said hi!

And to the three people who make my books look so good, Vivek, Connie, and Tom – my thanks to each of you for all you do for me.

And to all of you who ever wondered how fraudulent art scams work, enjoy the book. I learned so much when I wrote it. Hope you learn as much when you read it!

Win FREE Paperbacks every week!

Go to www.dianneharman.com/freepaperback.html and get your FREE copies of Dianne's books and favorite recipes immediately by signing up for her newsletter.

Once you've signed up for her newsletter you're eligible to win three paperbacks. One lucky winner is picked every week. Hurry before the offer ends!

PROLOGUE

"Will you be home for dinner this evening, darling? I can cook your favorite meal, lamb tagine."

Philippe Germain looked up from his morning newspaper at his wife, Simone, and frowned. "I think you meant to say you would have our long-suffering housekeeper, Dolores, cook it, right? It doesn't matter. Whatever's easiest for you to reheat later and pretend you made yourself, is fine with me." He reached for the roll of crusty French bread in the center of the table and tore off a chunk, smearing it with peanut butter. "Do you think I'm a complete idiot?" He chuckled to himself as several bread crumbs fell from the corner of his mouth. "It's just as well you have other talents, Simone, or I would have traded you in for a younger model long ago."

He leered at his wife's slender frame and generous cleavage which were accentuated by the tight-fitting plain black workout gear she was wearing. Reaching under the table, he ran his hand along her thigh, his eyes feasting on her perfect milky complexion. She wore her dark hair in a knot at the back of her head, and her flawless skin was free of any trace of makeup. Sparkling diamond studs in her ears were her only adornment. He'd never regretted his decision fifteen years earlier to bring her to America from France as his bride when she was only nineteen years old. "I'm just kidding, *chérie*, you know that, don't you?"

Simone's expression hardened as she pushed her chair out and stood up, avoiding his touch. "I hardly need to remind you I'm twenty years your junior, Philippe. How much younger were you thinking of?" The cold tone of her voice warned Philippe she was in one of her moods. It didn't bother him, because he knew from experience his wife wasn't a morning person. Simone was a lot friendlier in the evenings after a glass or two of wine and their two daughters were tucked away in bed.

He pretended not to notice her ill-temper. "Are you going to the gym this morning? You seem to be spending a lot of time there these days. Not that I'm complaining. You've never looked better."

Simone began to clear the breakfast dishes from the table. "What else do you expect me to do? You're away at the gallery all day, every day, and most of my friends have jobs. Now that the girls are old enough to take the bus to school, there's not much for me to do until they get home at four in the afternoon."

Philippe gave an exasperated sigh. "Let's not have this conversation again. It's getting old. I told you when we got married that I didn't want you to work. Your place is in the home, looking after me and our daughters." He paused. "And I might add, which you do very well, despite my jokes about your cooking."

Simone was leaning down to open the dishwasher, and she rolled her eyes when she looked up at Philippe, shaking her head. "Maybe if you were home more often we could be more like a proper family. You don't seem to even care that in a few more years Ava will be leaving for college. And Cecile can't wait to join the United States Air Force as soon as she turns eighteen." Simone made a sign of the cross with her right hand and mumbled a line of a prayer in French. "I wish you would have a word with her. Wherever she got the urge to become a helicopter pilot, I will never know."

Philippe took a large sip of his coffee. "I disagree. I like her spirit, and I think our daughter will do very well in the Air Force. She obviously wants to serve this great adopted country of ours. If you've got too much time on your hands, you should follow her example."

Simone straightened up and glared at her husband. "You want me to sign up for the military? I'd be surprised if you even noticed I was gone, considering how little attention you pay to me." She started wiping the white quartz countertop vigorously with a dish rag.

"Don't be ridiculous. You wouldn't last ten minutes without your designer shoes and Chanel purse. No, I meant you should do something useful with your spare time. It's a shame you're not eligible to join the Daughters of the American Revolution. The Cascade Chapter is very active here in Bellevue. They do great work." Philippe stared at the clock above the stove and jumped up. It was almost 8:00 a.m. His earlier walk with Aslan, their Newfoundland dog, had been farther than usual and thrown off his schedule. "I can't believe it's that late. With all this talking, I'm running behind." He drank the last of his coffee and stood up, striding into the hallway where he stopped in front of a giant gilded mirror and looked admiringly at himself.

Simone followed him, still holding the dish rag. Her face was flushed. "You know perfectly well why I can't join the Daughters of the American Revolution. I'm French, with no connections to anyone who fought for American independence. The only reason you want me to do some type of patriotic work is for your own gain. You just want to sell more of your overpriced paintings to rich old ladies who bake cookies for soldiers' care packages."

Philippe pulled on a black pea coat and reached for a slim gray cashmere scarf, which he twisted around his neck and tucked under his collar in a cravat style. "Whatever you say, my dear." He knew better than to argue with Simone once she started on one of her rants. Selecting a black beret from the coat rack, he tilted it on his head with both hands as he moved it around to find just the right angle.

Simone narrowed her eyes and looked at Philippe. "Why do you insist on wearing a stupid beret everywhere you go? And a scarf, carefully color coordinated to go with the rest of your outfit. Ha! You act so American, but you still like to look French, *non*?"

In response to Simone's comment about his attire, Philippe looked down with approval at his shiny, pointed black leather shoes, dark gray skinny pants, and cobalt blue sweater. A gold cross on a chain was visible around his neck, a gift from his mother on the day he'd left his home town of Saint-Victor-la-Coste, France, to seek his fortune in America. He'd taken only a small bag of belongings with him, a modest amount of cash which was an inheritance from his grandfather, and the cross signifying his family's blessing. He'd never removed the cross and chain from around his neck since that day.

Stealing one last look at his reflection in the mirror, Philippe turned around and smiled at his wife. "I'm very happy with my signature style, my darling. I'm just giving my clients what they want. They like dealing with an authentic Frenchman who looks the part. It's called branding." Seeing that Simone had opened her mouth and was about ready to start speaking again, he hurriedly reached for his briefcase and headed for the door. "I do value your opinion, my love, but I'm running late. I'll try to be back for dinner. *Au revoir.*"

Simone's parting insults were lost as the door closed behind him, and he hurriedly walked across the narrow, brick paved driveway to where two shiny, white, late model Mercedes were parked. The compact GLA SUV was Simone's, while Philippe preferred the sleek lines of his E-Class coupe. Jumping in, he quickly drove through the gates and away from his Bellevue residence, heading for his art gallery located in downtown Seattle.

It was a whistling Philippe, who a short time later, unlocked the heavy front doors to The Germain Plein Air Art Gallery in Pioneer Square. When he originally founded the gallery, he primarily featured Washington plein air artists. They were artists who worked outdoors and painted landscapes. After he'd acquired several Southern California plein air paintings from the early 20th century and had put them up for sale in his gallery, he discovered his clients preferred the ocean scenes and landscapes of a warmer, less rainy, climate.

That genre proved to be the most popular among his clients, and those paintings provided a vivid and colorful display in the gallery. As a result, he found himself spending a lot of time searching for

Southern California plein air paintings listed for sale by auction houses or by individuals in Southern California.

Philippe's footsteps echoed on the fake brick flooring as he strode into the wide-open gallery display area. He'd had the brick installed to give the impression of an old French cobbled street, something for which Simone had mocked him over the years. The main part of the gallery space was minimalistic with plain white walls, which drew a customer's eye to the artworks hung in gold frames on the wall. Simone may have scoffed at the French feel of the gallery, but Philippe's formula had worked very well. Business had never been better, and the gallery could barely keep up with demand.

He'd developed a reputation for finding paintings that were of an extremely high quality, and his competitors had accused him of ruining the market by overpaying for his acquisitions. Either that, they said, or his profit margins must be wafer-thin. But Philippe didn't seem to have any money problems, as his large gated house in an affluent area of Bellevue proved. He left his competitors scratching their heads while his customer waiting list grew longer each month.

On this particular morning, he carried out his usual routine of walking around the gallery, turning on the lights and straightening the paintings. Promptly at 9:30 a.m. a young woman entered the gallery. She greeted Philippe with a smile and the French custom of a kiss on both cheeks.

"Good morning, Renee," Philippe said. His part-time assistant, Renee LaPlume, was a student at the University of Washington. She worked at the gallery on the days when she wasn't attending her History of Art classes. "I'd like you to dust the frames of the paintings. I'm going to do some work in my office."

He sauntered off to the back of the gallery. The office, restroom, and storage area were located behind a blue fabric drape dotted with yellow flowers and stripes, hung from a rod. Philippe loved the nod to the Provence, France, style of his upbringing. It was something else he and Simone disagreed upon. She thought the French style of the gallery was a bit over the top, and she rarely made an appearance there.

Philippe spent the morning contacting customers, researching upcoming auctions, and dealing with paperwork. Renee stuck her head through the office door at noon.

"I will be going, Philippe," she said with a shy smile. Not for the first time, Philippe wondered if the young woman had a crush on him, but he resisted the temptation to entertain any thoughts about cheating on Simone. And why would he, since Renee was certainly not as attractive as his wife. In any case, if Simone ever found out he played around while he was away from home, his life would be unbearable, not to mention the cost of a probable divorce.

Although Philippe had been tempted to stray in the past, he'd never acted on it, despite his French upbringing where mistresses were commonplace. The thought of losing half of everything he'd worked for if Simone found out and left him, was enough to keep him monogamous. Sometimes, the way his wife looked at him made him think she needed a reason to divorce him, but he had no intention of giving her one.

He made sure that the gallery was free of customers before quickly eating the lunch he'd brought from a nearby deli on the way in. At the same time, he searched for paintings listed for sale on the internet. A knock on the back door broke his concentration, and he rose from his desk to answer it. He was expecting a shipment of paintings he'd bought to be delivered that afternoon, so he wasn't surprised when he heard the knock.

Opening the back door of the gallery was the last thing Philippe Germain ever did. With a startled look on his face, he stared at the person standing on the other side of the transom holding a large knife that glinted in the outdoor light. Without a word, the unexpected visitor plunged the shiny blade into his chest with a violent thrust.

Philippe spluttered for breath. "You," he said, stumbling forward and falling to the ground. His glassy eyes looked up into the face of his assailant before permanently closing.. His final word was a whisper. "Why?"

A slow smile spread across the killer's face, who then proceeded to stab Philippe two more times to make sure he was dead. A trail of blood oozed from Philippe's body as it was dragged into the storage room by the killer, who then closed the door, cleaned up the blood in the hallway, and left the gallery by way of the back door.

CHAPTER ONE

Jake Rogers pulled the SUV up to the valet stand at SeaTac Airport and exhaled a relaxing big breath. He turned to his companion and grinned. "We made it, in fact we're early for the flight. Did you notice that every single traffic light was green? Just how I like it. Are you ready for your vacation, birthday girl?"

DeeDee Wilson, his girlfriend of over a year, returned his smile, her face lighting up. "For sure. I didn't expect to be spending the night of my fiftieth birthday flying to an unknown destination for a week with the man of my dreams, but I can't think of anything I'd rather be doing."

Jake's blue eyes twinkled, and he opened his car door, leaving the keys in the ignition for the valet. "In that case." He walked around to the passenger door and opened it for DeeDee. "If you'd like to come with me, let's get this adventure started."

DeeDee giggled and held her hand out to Jake. Smoothing the skirt of the swanky dress she'd been wearing for the friends' party they'd attended earlier that evening, she stepped out of the car like she was some kind of a movie star, which was exactly how she felt. From start to finish, it had been a day to remember.

Breakfast in bed with champagne served on a tray with a red rose—that was a first. Jake had been apologetic that the toast was a little burnt, but that just made her adore him all the more. Cracking open the top of her boiled egg with a knife, she gasped in delight when a trickle of yellow yolk oozed out. "Ooh. That's perfectly runny, just how I like it." She gave Jake an impressed nod.

Jake had puffed up with pride at his culinary prowess. And when Balto, her husky dog, had jumped up on the bed carrying a gift-wrapped package tied with a pink ribbon, she opened it to find the dress she was now wearing and which she had previously admired in the display window of an upscale boutique. DeeDee choked up. "I went back to the store to get it," she murmured, "and they told me they didn't have any more left in my size."

Jake beamed again. "That's because Balto bought it," he said. "Oh, and there's something else. Remember how I mentioned to make sure all your laundry was done, and to cancel work for a week?"

DeeDee screwed up her face. "Hmm, about that. A client has been begging me to cater a…" Seeing Jake's face cloud over, she burst out laughing. "Just kidding. I wouldn't dare." She took a bite of her toast, which was definitely on the crunchy side.

That was when Jake had instructed her to pack for a week. "We're leaving tonight after Cassie and Al's housewarming party. They offered to watch Balto while we're away. Oh, and don't forget your passport."

DeeDee tried to contain a squeal of delight. She looked across the bed at Balto, whose ears had pricked up. "You're looking pleased with yourself, Balto. You get to go on vacation too and hang out with your pal Al, huh? Aren't you lucky?" Balto wagged his tail as if he understood and then wandered off.

After a leisurely breakfast, she and Jake had taken Balto for a long walk on the beach beside her house on Bainbridge Island. When they returned, Jake left to take care of a few things before their trip.

"I'll pick you and Balto up at six," he promised, with a lingering kiss. DeeDee's lips tingled at his touch. "And get ready for more of those when I get you all to myself for a whole week," he said, before driving away with the car stereo blaring, singing at the top of his lungs.

"He'll get arrested one of these days for crimes against music," DeeDee said to Balto before she began to pack. She'd already made an appointment to have her hair and makeup done at the local salon, which resulted in an enjoyable afternoon of being thoroughly spoiled and pampered.

Now, at the airport, heads turned to stare at the attractive blond woman and the ruggedly handsome man who embraced her as she climbed out of the car. The valet was loading their luggage onto a cart. Jake looked at DeeDee's three large suitcases and his one small one, but restrained from making a comment.

DeeDee, reading his mind, began to protest. "You wouldn't tell me where we were going, so what do you expect? You know I like to make sure I have everything I'll need."

Jake tried to keep a straight face, and for once was unsuccessful. "I sure hope so." He tipped the valet and they walked into the terminal.

"It's the moment of truth," DeeDee said when they arrived at the Departures area, and they faced the line of check-in counters. Jake reached into his coat and pulled out the travel documents. His eyes never leaving DeeDee's, he silently handed her the tickets.

DeeDee was speechless for several moments, but the smile that suddenly spread across her face said a thousand words. She only managed to utter a few. "Marseille? Seriously? We're going to Marseille?"

Jake nodded. "Glad you approve. We have a layover in Paris for a couple of hours on the way, because there aren't any direct flights from Seattle to Marseille." He nodded towards the check-in counter for the Air France flight to Paris. "Shall we?"

DeeDee slipped her arm through Jake's as he wheeled the luggage cart towards the short line. When it was their turn, the clerk that greeted them couldn't have been more charming. DeeDee handed the man their tickets and passports, while Jake placed the suitcases on the scale. The reading on the scale kept rising, and DeeDee held her breath. Jake was lightly pinching her arm, causing her to playfully shake his hand away.

The Air France clerk placed the destination tags around the handles of the suitcases, and handed the boarding passes and other documents back to DeeDee without any reference to excess baggage. Instead, she heard the magic words she hadn't even dared to hope for.

"We have an upgrade for both of you this evening," the agent murmured with a smile. "To Business Class. Please make use of the complimentary refreshments in the lounge, and enjoy your flight."

"That's so kind, thank you," DeeDee said. Her face was aching from smiling so much. When they were a safe distance away from the counter, she threw her arms around Jake and kissed him on his lips. "I love you, Jake Rogers. This is going to be the best trip ever."

Jake laced his hand through hers as they followed the signs to the Executive Lounge. "I could get used to this," he commented as they entered and were greeted by the concierge. They settled in a private booth, and looked over the snack menu while DeeDee sipped on a cocktail and Jake downed a beer.

"I guess we won't be needing these," DeeDee said, fishing a plastic storage container from her carry on bag. She opened the lid, and Jake squinted at the contents.

"Sandwiches? You made sandwiches for us?" he asked in a puzzled voice.

DeeDee laughed. "I told you, I like to travel prepared. I wasn't sure if we'd get a meal during the flight. I guess I was wrong. I'll throw these away when we leave."

Jake frowned. "No way. Keep them, just in case I don't like what they serve us on the plane."

True to his word, on the plane Jake finished the three-course meal, as well as the sandwiches, then reclined his leather lounger into a bed, and slept for most of the next ten hours.

*****

DeeDee peered through the cabin window as the plane was preparing to land at the airport in Marseille.

"I'm glad you're awake, so you don't miss anything," she said, nudging Jake. "Will you look at this." She moved over so Jake could lean across her and look out the window. "I've never seen the Mediterranean, but I had no idea it was so big. There are so many commercial ships and cruise liners. I don't know why, but I thought it would only be big enough for a few yachts and sailboats."

Jake's eyes widened. "Wow. That's a lot of fancy yachts." He nuzzled in closer to DeeDee, who was moving around excitedly in her seat. She looked away from the window, and turned to Jake. "I think this is the best birthday present in the history of ever. Thank you," she whispered.

Jake smiled sleepily. "You're welcome. Do you have any more sandwiches? I slept through breakfast."

DeeDee raised an eyebrow. "No, they were all eaten by you. I wish I could sleep on a plane. I watched two movies and read half of my novel. Oh, and I was thinking, could we go to a Michelin-rated restaurant while we're in France? Pleeeease?"

"That'll teach me to take a sleeping pill." Jake rubbed his eyes with a grin. "I think I sleepwalked through immigration in Paris. Of course we can go to a Michelin restaurant. Dinner is always very much on my mind."

The plane hit the tarmac with a bump, and bounced before

coming back down while the pilot applied the brakes. DeeDee was out of her seat as soon as the seatbelt signs were switched off. "Quick, so we'll be first in the line to go through Immigration," she said, nudging Jake, who hurriedly followed her lead.

When they'd collected their luggage, DeeDee waited with the luggage cart while Jake went to the car rental desk. She noticed that the French women had a different air about them when she compared them to women from other parts of the world. She wondered if they were born with that aloof sense of confidence, and if they instinctively knew how to tie a scarf just so.

Jake returned, jangling an ancient set of car keys, and they walked outside the terminal to pick up the rental car.

"What is this thing?" DeeDee asked as they approached a small orange vehicle. The paintwork had faded from the sun, and it was covered in dents and scratches from what looked like a number of unsuccessful parking maneuvers. She looked at it, hesitating. "Do you think it's safe to drive? I'm not sure if the suitcases will fit in."

"Cute, isn't it? It's a Renault 4. I'll drive," Jake said. "It's only about ninety minutes to the place where we're staying. When we get there, we can get some sleep, and then we'll have dinner."

"Care to tell me more?" DeeDee asked, helping Jake squeeze one of her suitcases into the tiny trunk. They got it in, and put another one, along with Jake's smaller case, on the back seat.

Jake scratched his chin and eyed the rickety roof rack as a possible resting place for DeeDee's third suitcase. "Nope. It's a surprise," he said as he smiled at her. "Make yourself useful and hold this rack steady while I try and secure your suitcase to it, or you're going to have to decide which of your suitcases you want to leave behind."

DeeDee's mouth fell open. "We're not going anywhere without them. Here, let me help you."

CHAPTER TWO

An hour and a half later, Jake turned the car into a cobblestone driveway lined with trees. As they bumped along, DeeDee tried to smother a yawn. The only thing that had kept her awake during the last stretch of their trip was the excitement of seeing the dramatic scenery on the often steep and winding roads along the way, and the fact that the old car they were traveling in didn't allow for a very smooth ride.

"We're here, aren't we?" She looked over at Jake, who had rolled up his shirtsleeves and was driving with one elbow resting on the open window. The late afternoon sun was still strong, and the vehicle had no air conditioning. The windows had metal handles to wind them up and down. It reminded DeeDee how old she was, and that she could remember when cars weren't full of electric gadgets or a flashing display panel.

Jake turned to her and winked. "Sit tight. Any minute now and you'll see where we'll be staying while we're in Provence. I hope you like it."

DeeDee groaned as the car hit a pothole, and she was thrown around in her seat. "You know what the best thing is about turning fifty?" She let out a chuckle and went on without giving Jake a chance to reply. "I guess you do, seeing as you're a little older than me."

Jake changed gears with the stick shift that looked like a handle that pulled in and out of the plastic dash. "Only by a couple of years," Jake reminded her. "Not that anyone could tell from my boyish good looks." The lines around his blue eyes creased up as he smiled. "Anyway, what is the best thing about turning fifty? Tell me."

DeeDee paused, gathering her thoughts. "Somehow, I feel lighter inside, kind of free. It's like a weight has been lifted off of me. If I'd known getting older would feel this good, I never would have worried about it." She shook her head, gazing through the windshield at the long shadows cast by the trees, before turning back to Jake. "Why doesn't anyone ever tell you that? It's taken me fifty years to finally grow comfortable in my own skin, and be true to who I really am. Now, instead of putting everyone else first, I get to focus on me. It feels good, and I don't feel selfish."

Jakes blue eyes twinkled. "I guess we just have to figure this stuff out along the way. I'm glad you feel like that, because there's nothing more beautiful than a woman who's confident in herself. That's one of the things I love about you. The last couple of years have been rough for you, but you've come through it much stronger."

DeeDee knew Jake was referring to her divorce after a long marriage. When she'd gotten divorced, she'd moved to Bainbridge Island, which is located across Puget Sound from Seattle, and started a catering business, Deelish. She'd worked hard to get her business off the ground, and now it was at the point where it was doing well with an established clientele. Her other focus was making sure her relationship with Jake didn't suffer as a result. Finding her way had been scary at times, but it had been well worth it.

The car had reached the end of the line of trees, and the cobbled lane opened onto a wide expanse. DeeDee was momentarily speechless. She blinked a couple of times to make sure she wasn't seeing things. "Wow," she whispered.

In front of them was a large chateau situated on a knoll overlooking a deep gorge on one side. The walls surrounding the building were divided by two small columns at the front, joined by a heavy gate serving as an entrance. Behind the gate, DeeDee could just make out a blue door, similar to the many other blue doors she'd seen on the drive from Marseille. Apparently, it was an old tradition in Provence for a homeowner to paint a home's front door blue. A large, covered porch stretched across the front of the chateau, surrounded by a meadow of purple wildflowers leading to orchards and vineyards in the distance beyond.

The gate was built for small cars such as the one they were driving, but even so, DeeDee held her breath as they passed through the narrow opening. There was a scraping noise as the car brushed past the columns.

Jake grunted. "I don't think anyone will notice a few more scratches on this old thing," he said, before coming to a stop on the circular driveway in front of the chateau.

The blue door of the chateau swung open and an imposing older French woman accompanied by a younger man came out to greet them. The heavyset woman was wearing a thick navy dress with a blouse underneath, and her graying hair was swept up in a solid roll at the back of her head. "That must be *Madame* Durand, the owner," Jake said, raising an eyebrow at DeeDee. "We'd better be on our best behavior. She looks like a tough old battle-axe."

DeeDee gave him a warning look as they climbed out of the car. DeeDee's legs and back were stiff, and she rolled her shoulders to loosen up. Despite the amazing surroundings, all she longed for at that moment was a warm shower and a comfy bed. There would be plenty of time to explore later.

The woman spoke English in a deep, heavily accented tone. "Welcome," she said with a formal nod. "I am *Madame* Durand, and this is Andre. He will take your bags and show you to your room."

DeeDee shuffled from foot to foot, suddenly nervous in case Andre would be offended when he saw all the heavy suitcases. Then DeeDee remembered the conversation she'd just had with Jake, and her self-confidence returned. She was quite sure in a chateau as grand as this, Andre was used to guests with a lot more luggage than theirs. She straightened up and followed Jake's lead, shaking hands with *Madame* Durand and Andre. "We're so happy to be here," DeeDee murmured.

A friendly Andre spoke up. His English was much better than *Madame* Durand's. "Dinner is served at 8:00 p.m. with wine in the library beforehand. *Madame* and *Monsieur* Durand will be hosting it. If you are hungry, we can also arrange something for you to eat now."

Never one to refuse food, Jake started to say something, but DeeDee interrupted. "If we eat now, it would probably spoil our dinner. I think we'd just like to go to our room. We're both tired after our long trip. Right, Jake?"

Jake held out his hand for DeeDee's. "Right. As usual."

They followed Andre through the chateau, along wide hallways and up a winding staircase leading to their room. Paintings lined the walls, and DeeDee, with a background of working as a docent at SAM, the Seattle Art Museum, recognized them as being very high quality artworks. When they reached the door of their room, Andre stopped and said he'd be back with the luggage, and would knock when it was in the hallway outside their room.

The large and airy room was decorated in the traditional French provincial style. The oyster-colored walls and carpeting provided an opulent backdrop to the chair that was in a corner with a caned seat, cabriole legs, and simple scalloped carvings. The same swirling design was repeated on the chalk paint headboard of the king size bed and the dresser along one wall. A marble bust looked right at home sitting on top of the dresser. While it appeared no period detail had been overlooked, on closer inspection DeeDee decided that was probably because the items all appeared to be authentic and quite possibly original to the residence.

DeeDee walked across the room to where the open windows looked out onto the chateau's vineyards and olive trees, beyond which the hill fell away into a cliff, and then down to the gorge below. Her senses soared as she absorbed the wild and wooded view, and she leaned her head on Jake's shoulder with a sigh of contentment.

Jake was the first to speak. "DeeDee, can you believe this? It's even better than what my friend told me it would be like. I mean, how many acres of vineyards and olive trees do you think they own?"

DeeDee shrugged. "I have no idea, but I remember a friend from the Midwest once told me that you never ask someone how many acres of land they have or how many cattle they own, because it's considered rude. I assume the same holds here for vineyards and olive trees, and I wouldn't like to offend *Madame* Durand."

"Me neither, but if we don't grab a quick nap, we will offend them for sure by falling asleep at the dinner table," Jake said laughing. He walked over to the bed and lay down, his feet hanging off the end.

By the time DeeDee had explored the bathroom, and heard the knock on the door from Andre to signal that their suitcases had arrived, Jake's snores were audible from the bed. DeeDee was too exhausted to care. She'd lost count of how many hours she'd been awake, and was too befuddled to figure it out or calculate what time it was in Seattle. She got in bed beside Jake, and drifted off in a dream of vineyards, castles, and Michelin-rated restaurants.

When they woke up almost four hours later, it was almost 8:00, and they just had time to shower and dress before heading to the library. From the voices coming from there, it sounded like several other guests had already started enjoying the wine.

A short man with a combover and a considerable paunch approached them. He looked admiringly at DeeDee, taking in her sleek shift dress accessorized with a simple string of pearls.

"You must be DeeDee," he said, with a half-bow. "I am *Monsieur* Durand, but please, call me Franck." He extended his hand to DeeDee and Jake in turn. "We are so happy to welcome you to Provence. Would you like a glass of wine? All of our vineyards are organic."

DeeDee exchanged a look with Jake. Her first impression was that Franck and his wife made an odd couple, but as usual she deferred any judgment without first getting to know them better. "I'd love to try some organic wine, thank you," DeeDee said. "Would you suggest something?"

Franck nodded. "Of course. Red and white wines from Provence are known throughout the world by wine connoisseurs. I think you will find they are all excellent. Please, follow me." He led them to a sideboard which displayed the wines. Grenache, Syrah, and Mourvédre reds and rosés, along with Ugni Blanc and Rolle whites, were all being poured.

With Franck's assistance, they settled on a Mourvédre. "This is wonderful, Franck," Jake said, tasting the wine. "I've never had it before."

"My pleasure," Franck said, before leaving them to greet other guests who were entering the library.

DeeDee savored the earthy aroma of the wine before taking a sip. The soft red fruit flavors came to life when they hit her tongue. She raised her glass to Jake's and they clinked them together. "If this is the precursor to our time in Provence, it's off to a wonderful start. I love you, Jake Rogers."

Jake wrapped his arm around her waist and kissed her temple. "And I, you."

A short while later, *Madame* Durand announced dinner was being served in the dining room. DeeDee and Jake filed in with the other eight guests and their hosts. They were all seated at one long table, DeeDee next to Madame Durand on one side, and Jake on the other.

DeeDee marveled at the taste of the deceivingly simple dish of Provence cassoulet, freshly baked bread, and a salad that tasted as if it had been brought directly in from the garden just before they sat down for dinner. She turned to her hostess to compliment her on the meal. "*Madame* Durand, this is amazing. I'm a caterer in the Seattle area, and I don't think I've ever tasted food this fresh. Is it sourced locally?"

A glimmer of a smile passed across *Madame* Durand's face as she spoke. "We grow almost everything on our own property. What we don't produce here comes from local farmers' markets. There is one somewhere in the region every day. For example, for breakfast we use fresh eggs from our hens, local bacon, and our own fruit."

"I think I'm going to enjoy breakfast very much," DeeDee said, sipping her wine.

Jake leaned across to face *Madame* Durand and nodded. "Me, too."

Madame Durand seemed to be loosening up. Her English was pretty good once she got talking. "You can come and see the orchards and vegetable gardens in the morning. We even have, how do you say it…" She paused for a second, thinking of the word. "Quail. You know of it?"

DeeDee smiled and nodded, indicating that she understood. At the same time, she wondered if *Madame* Durand would share her cassoulet recipe. She decided to wait until they'd been there a few more days before asking.

"You will not eat better anywhere in Provence than at Chateau Durand," *Madame* informed her. "What else do you have planned during your stay here?"

"We're looking forward to visiting some of the art galleries and restaurants in the area, isn't that right, Jake?"

Jake, who was munching on the crusty bread, swallowed before answering. "For sure. Sorry, I think I'm in French bread heaven. *Madame* Durand, if there's some sort of bread award, you get it."

Madame nodded politely. "If you like art galleries, you should visit the *Germain Gallerie*. I think you will enjoy it, because they also have landscapes by American artists that are similar to the landscapes of Provence. For food, you must eat at *Henri's Boulangerie*, because it has been given two stars by the Michelin Guide."

"We will," DeeDee said, her eyes shining. A sudden wave of tiredness swept over her. Jake gave her a concerned look, and when they were finished with dinner they said their goodnights to their hosts and the other guests. Upstairs, DeeDee brushed her teeth and pulled on a nightgown before sinking into Jake's waiting arms.

"Let's unpack in the morning," DeeDee said, before turning out the light. "Did I mention how much I love this place? I can't believe we're really here. I kind of feel bad Balto's not with us to enjoy it too."

She could feel Jake's body shake with laughter. "Are you kidding? Balto will be having the time of his life at Al's place. I don't want to alarm you, but he might not want to come home with you when we get back to Bainbridge Island."

"Ssh," DeeDee scolded him. "Maybe I'll call Cassie tomorrow to check on him. She could put him on the line and we could say hi. Or, even better, we could FaceTime with him."

Jake chuckled and rolled over. "Sure. You do that, and I'll really know you've gone crazy at fifty. Goodnight, sweetheart."

"Night," DeeDee mumbled, still determined to get in contact with Balto when Jake wasn't around.

CHAPTER THREE

A continental breakfast buffet was laid out in the dining room when DeeDee and Jake went downstairs the next morning. The selection of breads, cereals, cold meats, pastries, cheese, fruit, and freshly squeezed juices made a vibrant and colorful display. The spread of food on the buffet table was complemented by the rays of golden sunlight streaming through the windows, casting a warm glow on the room.

"I can't decide whether to have orange or apple juice," DeeDee sighed. "Or cranberry. Talk about tough decisions."

"Grapefruit for me," Jake grinned, filling a small crystal goblet from a jug of cloudy yellow liquid. "What are these chocolate pastries?"

"*Pain au chocolat*," DeeDee said, reaching for one and putting it on a side plate. "They're chocolate croissants, straight from the oven. I think it's going to be impossible to resist the gourmet temptations we'll be encountering on this trip, so I'm not even going to try."

"That's my gal," Jake said, rubbing his chin. "I guess it's going to take me a while to get through all of this goodness, but I'll do my best. I think I'll start with some fruit salad."

"Make that two," DeeDee said, "and I'll order the coffee." She walked across the room to an open window table. Several other tables were occupied, and DeeDee recognized a few couples from dinner the previous evening. There was also what looked like a large family group that looked as if they'd just arrived.

Andre approached them wearing the same friendly smile DeeDee remembered. "Good morning, *Madame*," he said. "I hope you slept well and that everything was comfortable?"

"Yes, thank you, Andre. I slept like a baby. I do need some coffee to fully wake me up, so I don't miss any of this wonderful morning."

"Of course, *Madame*. And *Monsieur* Jake?"

Jake had appeared with two dishes of fruit salad, and he set one in front of DeeDee before sitting down across from her.

"*Monsieur* Jake will have coffee as well, please, Andre," Jake said with a grin. "*Madame* Durand was telling us last night about the fresh eggs and local bacon. I'd really love to try those as well. How about two eggs, scrambled?"

"I'll have the same," DeeDee said. "That sounds like a perfect start to the day."

Andre nodded. "Coming right up," he said, before moving away to serve another table.

"I think Andre and I are going to get along just fine," Jake said, putting his spoon into the medley of fruit. He lowered his voice. "I'm not so sure about *Monsieur* Durand. I think he might be a bit of a creep. Maybe that's why his wife looks so miserable."

"Ssh," DeeDee said, glancing around to make sure no one had overheard Jake. "I thought she was a lovely woman. I think she's just reserved. Her passion for the local area and its produce was obvious. I'd like to talk to her some more."

Andre brought the coffee, and DeeDee and Jake enjoyed a

leisurely breakfast of several courses, sampling a little bit of everything. When they were done, Jake groaned. "I think I've died and gone to cheese heaven," he said. "And it's not even 10:00 a.m. So, what's the plan for our first full day in Provence?"

A woman sitting at the table next to them spoke up. A rosy-faced brunette in her forties with frizzy hair, she was with a distinguished-looking older gentleman who had a shiny bald head and a kind face. "I hope you don't mind me interrupting," she said, "but I overheard you say it's your first day here. There are so many places to see, you won't know where to start. This is our second visit. What kind of things do you like? I'm Chrisann, by the way, and this is my husband, Bob. We're from Fort Worth."

"Pleased to meet you both," DeeDee said, as the couples shook hands. "I'm DeeDee, and this is Jake. We're from the Seattle area. I'm a caterer, so food is pretty high on my list of interests."

"And mine," Jake added, "although I'm not a caterer. I just have a vested interest in eating it."

Chrisann giggled, and began to rattle off a list of restaurants she and Bob had visited and would recommend. "There's *Restaurant de la Pyramide*, in a little village called Vienne. The village is full of historical architecture—old Roman buildings, cobblestone streets, and flowers everywhere. I think it's cute, don't you, Bob?"

Bob nodded in silence. DeeDee got the impression that Chrisann did most of the talking in their relationship.

"You've gotta go to Avignon," Chrisann went on.

"I've heard of it," DeeDee said. "From what little research I've done, it's one of the largest cities in Provence, right? The reason I'm interested is I learned it has lots of art galleries as well as restaurants. After food, art's another of my passions. I used to volunteer at an art museum. I don't get the chance to visit museums much anymore, and it's something I miss."

"In that case, you'll love it," Chrisann said. "Go to *Ginette et Marcel* for lunch. Believe me, you won't regret it."

Chrisann also told them about *Brasseries George Restaurant* in the city of Lyon, which had one Michelin star. She explained Lyon was less picturesque than the countryside with lots of big city traffic. Then there was *Chez Feraud,* in a place called Aix-en-Provence, and *L'Atelier de Lean Luc Rebanel* in Arles, where Van Gogh painted.

"If you decide to go to any of those places, let me know," Chrisann said. "I'm a Modern Languages teacher, and I spent a year in Lyon as part of my college studies, so I can fill you in on some background."

"We'll take you up on that," DeeDee said, when Chrisann finished her monologue. DeeDee was interested in getting more information about the area. As well as being knowledgeable, Chrisann was a lively conversationalist, even if it was hard to get a word in edgewise. "I think we're going to take a walk through the beautiful grounds here, and then just stay local for today. We'll probably try *Henri's Boulangerie* in the village, which *Madame* Durand recommended, and take a look at the art on display at *Germain Gallerie.*"

"*Henri's* is something else." This, coming from Bob, startled DeeDee. He pulled his chair out and stood up with the aid of a cane. Chrisann rose and steadied him, taking his other arm.

"Well see you guys later," Chrisann said. "Have fun."

Jake reached across the table and put his hand on top of DeeDee's, giving her a warm smile. "We will."

*****

The April morning sunshine was warm enough to stroll through the grounds of the chateau without a coat, although in the shade of the orchard it was a little cooler. The sight of a covey of the cute quail running through the olive trees made DeeDee try to snap a photo of them with her cell phone camera, but they were too quick for her to catch a good shot. Somehow, Jake managed to insert himself in most of the pictures.

"We'll have to get Andre to take a few of us together later," DeeDee said with a laugh. "Or the photo album of our trip to Provence will be full of pictures of you. And I don't mean that in a bad way," she added hastily before Jake could think of a smart comeback answer. "For some reason, those little quail make me think of Julia Child. I must remember to check my copy of her *'Mastering the Art of French Cooking'* book when we get back to see if there are any quail recipes. I think I remember one for roasted quail with liver canapés."

Jake put his arm around DeeDee's waist. "Speaking of food, let's take a walk around the vineyards and work up an appetite for lunch. Then we can head into the village and hit *Henri's Boulangerie* before doing a bit of gallery hopping."

DeeDee wriggled out of Jake's grasp. "Sure," she said, running ahead. "It must be at least an hour since you've eaten. How will you ever survive?"

Jake sprinted after her. DeeDee had just about made it as far as the end of the orchard before he caught up with her and ensnared her with a bear hug and a kiss. "That," he said solemnly, stroking her hair, "is what you will get if you keep mocking me."

"In that case," DeeDee murmured, tilting her head back up to his and feeling herself melt into the deep pools of blue that were his eyes, "I guess this week is going to keep on getting better." She pulled away with a giggle and ran off again. "Race you to the vineyard," she yelled, knowing full well it wouldn't be long until he caught up with her for a repeat performance. And so it continued until they arrived back at the chateau an hour or so later. They went directly to their room and got ready to go into the village for lunch.

Saint-Victor-la-Coste was only a short drive down the hill from the chateau, its medieval buildings still intact and dominating the skyline, just as they had for hundreds of years. The small village center was scattered with a few typical types of village shops, and *Henri's Boulangerie* was easy to find, a traditional café-restaurant with a wooden-floored outdoor terrace situated beneath several large, shady trees. It was opposite the town hall, in front of which stood a large fountain and obelisk, and it served as the centerpiece of the village square, *Place de la Mairie*.

"It's called the Centenary Revolution Fountain," DeeDee said as they stood facing it. She was reading from a local guide book Andre had given her when they'd left the chateau. "Otherwise known as the Fountain of Knowledge. According to this, the fountain was restored in 1889 during a restoration of the village. The tall obelisk is dedicated to science and the metric system, and displays the names of Galileo and Newton."

Jake raised a hand to his forehead to shield his eyes from the sun, trying to make out the etchings on the different faces of the obelisk. "What's the writing on the sides? It looks like math equations."

"That's right," DeeDee said, scanning the text of the guide book. "It's different arithmetic and geometric principles. When it was constructed, the architect stated the fountain would quench our thirst in two ways: with water and knowledge."

"I know another way to quench our thirst," Jake said, pulling her by the hand toward *Henri's*. "Let's sit outside on the terrace with a beer and see what else the book says about this quaint little place."

DeeDee skipped the beer and had a cool glass of chardonnay white wine while they feasted on shrimp bisque with shaved fennel, freshly baked bread, and an apple salad. The bread was served with butter and a ramekin of Camargue salt, something DeeDee filed away in her head as a simple but unusual idea for her catering business. Despite her best efforts, and having cut down on work the previous few months to spend more time with Jake, her mind was never truly switched off when it came to recipes and food.

After lunch, they visited a couple of ancient churches before wandering from one gallery to another. It was late afternoon by the time they entered *Germain Gallerie*, the tinkle of a small bell above the door announcing to the owner that customers had entered the shop.

DeeDee was immediately captivated by the paintings on display. Having been a docent at the Seattle Art Museum for several years, she'd been exposed to a lot of very fine art. While she didn't consider herself to be an expert, she knew when a painting was good. The standard of the artwork displayed in this gallery was very high indeed.

The gallery featured numerous twentieth century oil paintings. The landscape of the Provence area was prominent in a number of pieces depicting rolling hills with picturesque vineyards and olive groves. In addition to the landscape paintings of Provence, there were also a number of paintings that DeeDee remembered were referred to as plein air art or California Impressionism.

"These are amazing," she whispered to Jake, slowly walking around the room. "There are pieces here by the American artists Hanson Puthoff, Alfred Mitchell, and Edgar Payne. I wonder how they ever got here."

Jake shrugged. "I know I can't tell a good one from a bad one, but I know what I like. Some of these, I like a lot. They don't seem too expensive, either."

The low prices were another thing puzzling DeeDee, who had done a rough exchange rate conversion in her head of the prices that were displayed in euros, back into US dollars. She told herself she must be wrong. Before she could work it out using the calculator on her phone, a large bearded man wearing a paint-smeared apron over a t-shirt and jeans appeared through the draped doorway which separated the gallery from his studio. He wore a diamond stud in one ear, and his tan arms were splashed with daubs of colored paint.

"Hello," the man said, wiping his hands on his apron. "I'm Marc Germain, the owner. Do you see anything you like?"

DeeDee was looking at a painting by Alfred Mitchell, a large landscape with a barn and hills in the background that was mounted in a gold frame. She knew she'd seen it before, and was trying to recall where. Racking her brain, she realized with surprise it wasn't from an exhibition or the Seattle Art Museum. She remembered her friend, Cassie, had recently bought an almost identical painting from a gallery in Seattle. DeeDee had seen it just a couple of days beforehand hanging in the hallway of Cassie's new home on Bainbridge Island, and she'd admired it at the time.

DeeDee turned to Marc. "Could you tell me where this is from? It looks kind of familiar."

Marc smiled. "My uncle in Seattle owns an art gallery and sends plein air paintings to my gallery. Since this type of American art is very similar to the Provence landscapes, they sell quite well here in this part of France. It's a popular style, which is probably why it looks familiar."

Something was still bothering DeeDee. On closer scrutiny, she thought the brushstrokes and the artist's name were slightly different from the one Cassie had recently purchased.

"I'm really interested in this one," DeeDee said, ignoring Jake's look of surprise. "There are a few others I like as well. Would you mind if I take a couple of photographs with my camera, and think it over?"

"Of course, that's not a problem," Marc said with a nod. "Please, go right ahead."

The sound of the bell ringing above the door indicated more customers had arrived, and Marc went to greet them.

Jake spoke to DeeDee in an urgent whisper. "We'll never fit it on the plane going home. We need to leave before you do something crazy like buying it."

DeeDee raised a warning finger to her lips, and Jake became silent. He waited until she'd finished taking several photos and they were outside before he said anything more on the subject. "DeeDee, what was that all about? I can tell when you're up to something. And I have a funny feeling it has nothing to do with you buying that painting. Am I right?"

They quickened their steps back towards their car.

"Yes," DeeDee said. "That's because it's almost exactly like the one Cassie bought, but the brush strokes and the signature are a little different."

Jake thought for a second. "It can't be. You must be imagining it. I know the one you're talking about at Cassie and Al's place, but it's just similar, that's all. Like the guy said, it's a popular style."

DeeDee was adamant. "Jake, I know it sounds crazy, but I have an eidetic memory. I don't talk about it much because when I was a young child, people thought it was weird. My sister, Roz, used to tease me so much I developed a complex about it. I've never mentioned it to you before, because there was no reason to."

"So, what does having an eidetic memory mean? Is it something like a photographic memory?"

"Exactly," DeeDee said. "I have total recall when it comes to images. That's one of the reasons why I've always liked art so much. I can recall an image so vividly in my mind that it appears to be real."

Jake scratched his head. "Oh, dear," he said, taking the car keys out of his pocket. "I think I can feel a mystery coming on."

CHAPTER FOUR

During the week that followed, DeeDee and Jake settled into a relaxed routine of romantic springtime strolls and gastronomic delights. The smell of the Provence countryside became familiar to DeeDee, the breeze carrying with it a fragrance unlike any other she had known, a mix of piney shrubs, spicy herbs, and sweet flowers. The scent followed them as they explored the local region, visiting towns and restaurants that were either recommended to them or they came across by chance, just stopping when they liked the look of a place. They basked in the sunshine and flavors and irresistible aromas of Provence, exploring sprawling outdoor markets, and roaming dusty streets. The taste of the lush wines they sampled along the way only added to the idyllic trip.

One day, while exploring the countryside, they found themselves in the small village of Vienne. It was clear why architects considered the village to be the Holy Grail, due to the Roman influence still evident in temple ruins, a variety of churches with different architectural styles and an incredible statue of St. Peter. As they ambled along the narrow cobblestone streets, floral containers hanging from every window decorated their path with brightly colored geraniums in lavenders, reds, and whites spilling out of them.

"We have to eat here, it's the place Chrisann told us about," DeeDee had insisted when they caught sight of *Restaurant de la Pyramide*, and as she peered through the windows. The village's floral theme was continued inside, with bouquets of flowers everywhere in the restaurant. They feasted on the market lunch, which was a cheese platter with three kinds of cheese, a buttery brie, a bold Etorki, and a classic blue Roquefort. It came with freshly baked bread, crunchy nuts, and slices of sweet pears and cantaloupe. Even Jake had to admit his appetite was satisfied when they finished eating.

"Thank goodness your French is pretty good," Jake commented over an espresso after their meal. "Otherwise, I'd have no idea what to choose from the menu in all these amazing places. I'm learning more about you all the time. How did you pick it up?"

"I had a pen pal when I was younger, a girl named Magalie from a seaside town on the western coast of France called Les-Sables-d'Olonne. We wrote to each other for years," DeeDee said, adding cream to her coffee. "She wrote to me in French, and I wrote to her in English. When we were teenagers, she came to stay with my family one summer. We became such good friends that we spent alternating summers at each other's homes for the next four years. We lost touch when we both got married. I often wonder what happened to her."

"That's nice," Jake said, reaching for DeeDee's hand across the table. "I'm sure she thinks of you too."

In Lyon, a city further north, they dined at *Brasseries George Restaurant*, rated with one Michelin star. Lyon was less picturesque than the countryside with its heavy city traffic, although DeeDee enjoyed seeing *Place Bellecour*, the gigantic dusty red pedestrian square right in the middle of the city center. Surrounded by linden and cherry trees along with beautiful Napoleonic buildings, the square's centerpiece was a statue of the Sun King, Louis XIV, on horseback.

Another day, on a trip to Valence, they ate at *Pic le 7*, a rare three-star Michelin restaurant. When she tasted the dish she had ordered, a Provence specialty called *pan bagnat*, DeeDee groaned with delight. "If only I could replicate this for Deelish," she said to Jake, letting him sample a bite. "It looks so simple, but it's executed to perfection."

The *pan bagnat* was a type of open-faced sandwich with tomatoes, green beans, tuna, and sliced hard-boiled eggs tossed in a light vinaigrette dressing served on a toasted split sourdough roll and covered with lightly fried anchovies. When Jake tasted it, he agreed. "For once, I approve of you taking notes while we're at a restaurant," he said, as DeeDee snapped photos with her cell phone and scribbled down ingredients in the notebook she carried everywhere. "If you can recreate this back at home, I'm yours for life."

Dessert was another specialty of the region, *Gateau labally*, an orange blossom scented brioche with pink pralines, which sent Jake into even more raptures.

They left the chateau early on the day they drove to Avignon, one of the largest cities in Provence, and known for its art and restaurants.

"I want to make sure we have plenty of time to see everything," DeeDee explained along the way. "Did you know Avignon was the seat of the papacy in the 14th century?"

Jake looked confused. "I thought the Pope lived in Rome?"

"Usually that's the case," DeeDee said, referring to her travel guide book. "But Pope Clement V, a Frenchman, refused to move to Rome when he was elected. For the next sixty-seven years there was a papal community in Avignon, and seven successive popes lived there, too."

"I can guess what's coming next," Jake said, looking at DeeDee out of the corner of his eye. "I bet the town has a lot of churches. Is that the theme for today?"

DeeDee smiled. "Kind of. There are numerous minor churches, but the two best known monuments are the *Palais des Papes* and the *Notre Dame des Doms*. It says here that both of them overlook the city and are a must-see for all tourists. How about if we look at those two and then find the place for lunch Chrisann recommended?"

Jake nodded. "Sure, sounds like a plan. The restaurant she told us about in Aix-en-Provence was wonderful. I trust her judgment."

DeeDee recalled the meal Jake was referring to at *Chez Feraud*. They had dined on a dinner of *pistou* soup, a Provencal version of minestrone, grilled lamb, warm figs, and for dessert, caramel ice cream. They washed it down with a fabulous Rhone wine. She hoped she never was asked what meal she'd enjoyed the most over the past few days, but that one was certainly high up on the list.

They found a parking space, and made their way on foot to the breathtaking *Palais des Papes*. The largest Gothic palace in Europe, it was as big as four normal Gothic cathedrals. Rising above the city and the Rhone river, the walls of the palace were flanked by four mighty towers. With more than twenty rooms open to the public, they took their time meandering through its historic stone hallways and steps. The pope's private chambers and the priceless frescoes in the interior chapels painted by the Italian artist Matteo Giovannetti were of particular interest to DeeDee.

Nearby, the cathedral *Notre Dame des Doms* was small in comparison to the *Palais des Papes*, but still an imposing structure. Flooded with light, the marble stonework had been recently restored. Under the huge hexagonal dome, many sculptures and paintings were on view, alongside two organs, a 12th century marble throne used by the Popes, and a treasure of religious objects, reliquaries and vestments in the chapel devoted to John XXII.

Ginette et Marcel was the place Chrisann had recommended for lunch, where they each devoured an open-faced goat cheese and honey sandwich, called a *chevre miel tartine*. Once again, DeeDee started to scribble in her notebook.

"Does your memory recall extend to food as well?"

DeeDee knew Jake was teasing her.

"Maybe that's why you're such a good cook," he added. "Because you can memorize the flavors and create them after you taste them."

"It does help," DeeDee admitted. "Even though I don't talk about it, I guess it's something I use constantly for Deelish. When I try to recreate something I've tasted before, I know immediately if it's not quite right. The ingredients might all be there, but the proportions may be wrong. I try to tweak it until it works."

She sipped on her wine, while Jake looked at the road map and they planned the itinerary for their trip to Arles the following day.

In Arles, the city where Van Gogh painted, they explored the Roman ruins before loitering in the open-air market. Lunch was at *L'Atelier de Lean Luc Rebanel*, a Michelin-rated restaurant featuring local food of the season.

"I think I'll remember every place we visited on this trip by what we ate there," DeeDee said as the waiter served the Bistro salad, which consisted of several kinds of greens and bacon mixed with a light dressing, and topped with a poached egg.

They followed it with raspberry tart for dessert, which Jake summed up in one word. "Historic."

From Arles, they made their way to the small commune of Les Sainte Maries de la Mer on the Mediterranean Sea, a thirty-minute drive away. On the way to the *Notre Dame de la Mer* church, they were panhandled by a number of gypsies.

"There's a story about that," DeeDee said as they walked past them. "The gypsies' patron saint, Sarah, the Black Madonna, has a crypt in the nave of the church. I was reading about it in the car on the way from Arles."

"Go on," Jake said, clasping DeeDee's hand. "Tell me the story of the Black Madonna. I'm sure you're going to, anyway."

DeeDee grinned. "Yep. According to legend, she was the black assistant who accompanied Mary Magdalene, Mary Salome, and Mary Jacobs to France when they fled the Holy Land after the crucifixion. Supposedly they were in a small boat, and she helped them land safely. It's a legend, and no one knows if the story of the Black Madonna is true. Next month this town is supposed to be filled with Roma gypsies. They arrive to honor Saint Sarah in May. They come about a week before the scheduled ceremony so they have time to socialize, arrange marriages, and celebrate baptisms."

After visiting the church, they walked along the seafront, stopping for coffee and ice-cream. DeeDee picked up a refrigerator magnet for her daughter, Tink, which had become a tradition every time she went on a trip. Despite the fact Tink was turning twenty-three, DeeDee knew she didn't dare go home without one.

"Maybe we could come back again to Provence," Jake said, reading her mind. "It would make a nice honeymoon destination."

DeeDee gripped his hand tighter. "It would," she said, smiling and raising her lips to meet his. "Let's sleep on that, but first, let's decide what we're going to do tomorrow, which is our last day here in Provence. Maybe lunch at *Henri's* before we take off for the airport?"

Jake met DeeDee's eyes, and his gaze flooded hers with love. "That would be perfect."

Soon they arrived back at their car and climbed in. The exhaust pipe rattled when Jake drove off, and DeeDee rolled her window down by winding the metal handle. "I'm going to miss this old heap of junk," she said, settling back in the seat, which no longer gave her a crick in her neck. Now, it seemed like it was almost made for her.

CHAPTER FIVE

When they touched down at SeaTac Airport the following evening, DeeDee was exhausted. The time difference between Marseille and Seattle meant that although it was a fifteen-hour trip, her watch was saying she'd left France in the afternoon and arrived back in the United States only a few hours later.

Despite them not receiving an upgrade on their homeward trip, Jake had once against demonstrated his ability to fall asleep anywhere. He took a sleeping pill and reclining in his Premium Economy aisle seat, fell asleep almost instantly. While he was sleeping, DeeDee had spent a long time updating her recipe notebook with the different dishes they'd eaten in Provence, occasionally nudging Jake from time to time when his snores reached embarrassing decibel levels.

The picked up their car at the valet stand and the familiar ferry ride to Bainbridge Island, followed by the short drive to DeeDee's house, were comforting. DeeDee was glad Jake had opted for the valet service, although she was sure it had been expensive.

"I had an amazing week in Provence," DeeDee said, stifling a yawn, "and although I didn't want to leave, I really am looking forward to sleeping in my own cozy bed tonight, even if it's not in a fancy chateau. And I can't wait to see Balto. I wonder if he missed us."

"Unlikely," Jake said, as they pulled into DeeDee's driveway. "After all, you FaceTimed him almost every day. Don't think I didn't know what you were up to on those sneaky calls before dinner while I was in the bathroom."

DeeDee opened her mouth to protest, but changed her mind and decided to come clean. "I admit I may have checked in with Cassie to speak with Balto a couple of times," she said with a smile. "I called my sister Roz as well, and my daughter, Tink. Balto's part of the family just as much as they are. I could hardly leave him out, could I?"

As they climbed out of the car, Jake cocked his ear. Balto's barks could be heard from the yard at the back of the house.

"That was thoughtful of Cassie and Al to bring Balto home when we called them from the airport," Jake said. "I like having them live nearby. You go see your beloved pet, and I'll take our bags in the house."

DeeDee walked across to where Jake was standing, looking at her with a grin. Away from the daily distractions of work, the trip had served to bond them with an extraordinary closeness that had surprised her, even though things were already going well between them.

She placed her arms around his neck, pulling him close. "Thank you, Jake, for the most wonderful week in Provence." Her lips hovered close to his. "You're my beloved, you do know that, don't you?" She kissed him lightly. "But I don't want Balto to feel neglected. See you in a few minutes."

She started to break away from their embrace, but Jake held her tightly to him. Staring into her eyes, he brushed a strand of hair off her cheek. "Wait. I have a question for you. I know we talked before about this…thing, and it was something neither of us was sure if we wanted to do again."

DeeDee held her breath, and a strange sense of calm washed over her. A few months earlier she would have rushed away from a conversation like this in a blind panic. "Go on," she whispered, holding Jake's gaze.

Jake reached up and removed her arms from around his neck, and fell down onto one knee. His eyes were shining, and DeeDee choked back a tear.

"DeeDee Wilson," Jake said. "You are the woman of my dreams. My heart, my soul, my everything. I can't imagine being without you. I want to grow old with you. And Balto, of course. Will you marry me?"

DeeDee's stomach flipped, and she gulped.

"You don't have to give me an answer now," Jake went on. "Think it over for as long as you want. And if you'd rather not get married, that's fine with me too. I just want you to know there is nothing that would make me happier than to call you my wife."

DeeDee held her arm out to Jake, and pulled him up.

"Of course, it's yes, you idiot," she said, and he started to smother her forehead, cheeks, and then her lips with tiny kisses. Balto barked in the distance. "You already make me feel like the happiest woman alive. I'd be honored to marry you, Jake Rogers. Yes, yes, yes!"

"I love you more than words can say," Jake whispered, giving her one last kiss. "We've got plenty of time to work out the details. Now go see Balto, while I get this stuff inside."

DeeDee felt like she was floating on air as she went around the side of the house to the back where Balto was running around in circles in the fenced area of the yard.

It was typical of Jake, she thought, *to propose to her in the driveway, when he had his choice of any of the fancy restaurants they'd dined in the past week. He wore his heart on his sleeve, saying what he thought whenever it came into his head, and wherever that happened to be.*

And for DeeDee, his driveway proposal was the most romantic moment she'd ever experienced.

"C'mere, my best boy," she said, opening the gate. Balto bounded over, and she rubbed his black and white fur, crouching down so his face was level with hers. His one blue eye and one brown eye stared back at her. "Don't tell Jake I said that," she whispered as Jake opened the kitchen door, and Balto followed her out of the yard and into the house.

"Hey, fella," Jake said when they entered. Balto went over to Jake and allowed himself to be petted, before settling back at DeeDee's feet. So, it's like that, is it?" Jake said, with a chuckle. "I can see I'm going to have to fight for Balto's affections again after his vacation with Al, but I think you've still got the number one place in his heart, DeeDee."

DeeDee shrugged at Jake, and smiled down at Balto. "Flattery will get you everywhere. I think Balto will be hungry soon, and he's probably not the only one. Am I right?"

Jake laughed. "You might be. But there's no way my wife-to-be is cooking after the long day we've had. I'll take Balto down to the beach, and see if I can wheedle my way back into his good graces. You take it easy and when I get back, I'll take care of Balto's food and water, and we can order takeout."

"You know what?" DeeDee said, wandering into the hallway where the light on the answering machine indicated she had several messages. "That sounds wonderful. After a week of Michelin-starred meals, I have a craving for pizza."

"You got it," Jake said, stopping for a lingering kiss as he picked up Balto's leash from the hallway table. He was interrupted by a woof from Balto, who had brushed past them and was waiting impatiently at the front door, wagging his tail. "Yes, Balto, I'm coming," Jake muttered, heading to the door while DeeDee pressed the flashing button on the answering machine.

She checked her messages, making notes about several people who were inquiring about catering events.

She smiled when the machine beeped and her sister Roz's voice came on the line. "Hey, Sis, are you back yet? You must be if you're listening to this." DeeDee rolled her eyes. "I want to hear all about your trip. Call me as soon as you get this message. So that's right now, do you hear me? Call me. Now."

DeeDee skipped to the next message. If she called Roz and started telling her about the trip and that Jake had just proposed when they got back, she'd never get her off the line. DeeDee wanted to keep the proposal's warm and fuzzy feeling to herself for a little while longer. She was still processing it internally, and she wanted to have a discussion with Jake about their plans when he got back from his walk on the beach with Balto. That's if she could keep her eyes open.

She decided to return the calls the following day, with the exception of a couple that couldn't wait. She pressed a number on her cell phone, and walked into the great room where she settled onto the sofa. "Susie? Hi, it's DeeDee. We just got back, and I picked up your message about the cocktail party at Colin James' place tomorrow. Is everything under control?"

"Hey, DeeDee, welcome back. It's all good to go." Susie, her helper at Deelish, sounded out of breath. "I'm at Colin's house right now, seeing to some last-minute details. He wanted fairy lights strung around the pool area. I ordered extra outdoor seating and floral displays to make the place look pretty. I've just been moving a few things around. Colin said the budget's not an issue."

"Susie, you're an angel." DeeDee was grateful for Susie's enthusiasm and the great ideas she'd contributed to DeeDee's business. It had been Susie's suggestion for DeeDee to partner with other local businesses to provide premium event services such as décor and styling. Susie project-managed everything, the other suppliers did the work, and DeeDee and Susie split the commission on the additional services down the middle.

"The food's all prepped and ready to go in the van," Susie added.

"I hope you didn't do it all yourself," DeeDee said. "Was Kristen available to help?" Kristen was a student friend of Susie's, who did some casual waitressing work when DeeDee needed extra staff.

"Yes, and she's coming tomorrow night as well. I know you're probably wiped out, so all you need to do is show up at Deelish tomorrow, and drive the van to Seattle. I'll have it packed up in the morning and ready to go for you."

"It sounds like you've thought of everything," DeeDee said, thinking the refrigerated van she'd bought the month before was a godsend. The business was at the point where trying to cram everything into her SUV for the bigger events she was catering wasn't working. Her son, Mitch, an accountant with an international firm in Seattle, had crunched the numbers and assured her the van was a necessary and affordable business expense.

"The last-minute things can be done at Colin's home before the party," Susie went on. "Kristen and I will meet you there tomorrow evening. How was your trip by the way?"

DeeDee gave a lazy smile. "I'll tell you all about it tomorrow, Susie, I promise. Right now, I'm so tired I can hardly think straight."

"I'll be waiting to hear all about it," Susie said with a laugh, as DeeDee ended the call.

She rested her head back on the sofa to decompress after the long flight, and considered closing her eyes. She was tempted, except she was pretty sure she'd fall asleep. There was one more call she wanted to make. Picking up the phone again, she dialed Cassie's number.

Cassie's husband, Al, answered. "Yo," he bellowed into the phone.

DeeDee heard Cassie say something in the background.

"Hey, Al, it's DeeDee," she said. "I just wanted to thank you and Cassie again for watching Balto while we were gone."

"Don't mention it," Al said. "We had a great time, out in my sailboat every day. Balto sure loves boats, doesn't he? His enthusiasm is contagious."

"That's an understatement," DeeDee laughed. "Can I have a quick word with Cassie?"

"Sure, here she is," Al said. There was crackling on the line while he handed the phone to his wife.

"Hi, DeeDee. I've told Al not to answer the phone like that," Cassie said with a sigh, "but he says he's not a receptionist. Was Balto all right when you got back?"

"He was," DeeDee said. "Thanks again. I was actually calling about something else. This is a strange question, Cassie, but you know that Mitchell painting hanging in your hallway? I just wondered where you bought it."

"It's from the Germain Gallery in Seattle," Cassie said without skipping a beat. "They specialize in plein air paintings and have a lot of paintings of Southern California landscapes. The owner told me he sells a lot of them, because it's a very popular genre with Seattle art collectors. There are a number of plein air artists in Seattle, and people are really collecting that genre of art. Why do you ask?"

"It's funny, because we saw several in that genre on our trip," DeeDee said. "I guess I never realized how much I liked them. Jake wouldn't let me buy one while we were there, but would you mind if I stopped by tomorrow and looked at it again?"

"I'd love that," Cassie said. "You can tell me all about Provence when you're here. I'm practically a sailboat widow these days. It seems like Al is out on his new boat nearly all day every day. He's become great friends with our next-door neighbor, Dino Argyros, and if the two of them aren't out on the water, they're planning crazy things like an around the world sailing adventure."

DeeDee stifled a laugh. Nothing would surprise her when it came to Al De Duco. "I'll come over in the afternoon," she said. "I think I might have trouble waking up early tomorrow morning."

As she ended the call, she heard Jake and Balto climbing the steps of the front porch and waited for them to come in, trying to think of the last time she'd felt this happy.

CHAPTER SIX

The air was crisp when DeeDee walked Balto along the beach the following morning. Jake had brought her a cup of coffee when he'd left for work, but after kissing him goodbye she'd closed her eyes for a moment and immediately fell right back to sleep. The sound of Balto whining on the pillow beside her had finally roused her a little after 11:00 a.m.

"Okay, I get the message, Balto," she said, moving her head away from his doggie breath. "I think some fresh air would do both of us some good. Just let me take a quick shower."

DeeDee was still groggy after showering and pulling on some old sweats, but by the time she and Balto turned down the steep sandy path to the beach, she could feel her senses coming back to life. At the end of the path, she let Balto off his leash, and watched him frolic as he ran in and out of the water's edge.

DeeDee inhaled the salty air and stuffed her hands in her coat pockets, the only sound she could hear being the water lapping at her feet. A soft light breeze cooled her skin. From time to time, Balto would appear at her heels with a stick in his mouth, and she'd throw it into the distance and wait for him to come bounding back with it.

Her head was full of the wonders of her past week with Jake, and what she'd come back to when she returned from Provence. She'd started a new life on Bainbridge Island a year earlier, and now she found herself on the edge of another new adventure, getting married for a second time. To say Jake was the love of her life would have been disrespectful to her ex-husband, Lyle, with whom she shared two wonderful adult children.

When Lyle had an affair with his secretary and left DeeDee, she'd never imagined that she'd find happiness again with another man. But DeeDee believed in looking forward, not back, and time had healed the old wounds, so she no longer had bad feelings for Lyle. Jake was many things that Lyle was not, and she felt blessed that Jake had found his way into her life and loved her as fiercely and unconditionally as he did.

The thought of getting married again filled her with joy, excitement and hope, and she hoped her children and her sister would share her enthusiasm. She knew Cassie's daughter, Brianna, had initially been reluctant to accept Al into the family when her mother had remarried, but Cassie's circumstances were different.

Al had been with the Mafia for many years as a bodyguard and friend to a man named Vinny Santora. DeeDee had met both of them at Roz' wedding, because her husband was Vinny's nephew. Unfortunately, Uncle Vinny had been murdered at the reception, and shortly afterward, Al retired to the Cayman Islands.

His retirement had been short-lived when he'd come back to the Seattle area to protect DeeDee when she'd been targeted by a murderer. He'd met Cassie at DeeDee's home, they'd fallen in love, and subsequently gotten married. Brianna was now one of Al's biggest fans.

"Let's go, Balto," DeeDee yelled, her hands cupping her mouth. Balto turned, and she waved him toward her. "I have a lot to do before the party I'm catering tonight."

Balto hung his head, and followed her back up the path, lagging behind. "You're just like a sulky child," DeeDee scolded, waiting for him to catch up. He looked up at her, and her heart melted. "Don't give me those big, sad eyes, buster." She rested a hand on her hip. "Do you realize how much I missed you while we were away? Jake will take you back to the beach later, after I go out. Is that a deal?"

Balto walked past her with what looked like a doggie smile on his face, and DeeDee smiled to herself as she brought up the rear.

Back at the house, she powered up her laptop and returned the rest of the work-related messages she'd picked up from the answering machine the previous evening. While she was walking Balto, she'd gotten the idea to call a gallery she and Lyle had visited in Laguna Beach when they'd taken a trip to Southern California several years earlier.

She remembered when she was a docent at SAM, someone had returned from a trip there, and they'd talked about the wonderful art in the gallery. She recalled the owner's name, Kevin Morgan, and wondered if he could help with her questions about the painting she'd seen in Marc Germain's gallery in Saint-Victor-La-Coste.

She found the contact details for Morgan Galleries in Laguna Beach on Google, and pressed the number into her cell phone. The receptionist put her call through immediately.

"Hello, Mr. Morgan, my name is DeeDee Wilson. I live in the Seattle, Washington area. You probably don't remember me, but we met several years ago when my husband and I visited your gallery."

"I meet a lot of people," Kevin said in a friendly voice. "So please excuse me if I admit I can't place you, but it's always nice to hear from our visitors again. What can I do for you, Mrs. Wilson?"

"I have an odd reason for calling you," she began, "but I hope you can help me. I was recently at a gallery in Provence and saw a painting there that looked very similar to one a friend of mine bought here in Seattle a couple of months ago. I was wondering if you could tell by looking at a photo of the painting if there's anything that seems odd about it?"

"It's pretty hard to do that by just looking at a photo," Kevin said, "but I'd be happy to see if I can. I can't promise anything, though."

"That's fine, I completely understand," DeeDee said. "Where shall I send the photo? To the gallery email address?"

"It would probably be quicker if you send it to my cell phone," Kevin replied, giving her the number. "That way, I'll pick it up immediately. Do you mind me asking why you're questioning it?"

"I'm eidetic," she said. "I don't use my photographic memory often, but there's something about the painting I saw in France and the one my friend has that's bothering me. I wouldn't ask you to tell me if one of them is a fake or anything, I'd just be curious to get your thoughts on it."

Kevin paused before replying. "Is there any chance you could get a photo of the piece your friend bought, so I could compare them? Of course, you realize I can't make a firm judgment as to authenticity from photos, but I would like to see what has your curiosity aroused."

"Yes, I'll send it over a little later. I live on Bainbridge Island in Washington, and I have to attend an event in Seattle this evening, but I'm sure I'll have time to stop by my friend's this afternoon. I'll send both pictures to you at the same time. Thanks so much for taking my call, Kevin. I really appreciate your help."

"You're welcome," he said, and hung up.

DeeDee scrolled to Cassie's name on her phone. Cassie answered on the second ring. "Hi, DeeDee, I recognized your number. How's the jet lag?"

"I can hardly keep my eyes open. I was fine earlier, but now I'm not sure how I'm going to make it through the party I'm catering this evening. I just wondered if it would be all right if I stop by this afternoon?"

"Of course," Cassie said. "You know you're always welcome, but Al and I will only be at the house for the next hour or so because we're having our first sailing lesson in a little while."

DeeDee was confused. "I thought you said Al's been out on his sailboat every day?"

"Oh, he's been on it," Cassie said with a laugh. "But that doesn't mean he's actually done any sailing. The boat's tied up to the wooden dock at the end of the garden, and he sits there, reading, and talking to his dog, Red. When Balto was here, Al let the boat out as far as the length of the rope, and Balto sat with him while Al did some fishing. He says he's just getting used to being on the open water."

"Well, that's something," DeeDee said. "Baby steps." She suspected Al's enthusiasm for learning to sail had been overshadowed by his lifelong fear of water, and she admired him for trying to overcome it. "In that case, I'll be right over. See you in ten minutes."

DeeDee picked up her car keys from the hallway table. Balto, who was playing with his toy rabbit, looked up. "I'm going to see Cassie and Al…" She had been about to ask Balto if he wanted to come with her, but Balto had already bolted for the front door.

"I guess that's a yes," she laughed as she walked outside to her car and opened the door for him to jump in.

When DeeDee pulled into the driveway of Cassie's impressive waterfront home a short while later, she had to push the memory of the murder that had happened there out of her mind. Before Cassie and Al bought the residence, it had belonged to the popular New Day NW television entertainment presenter, Dana Donnelly. Dana had been stabbed to death next to the pool house the previous New Year's Eve, following a party DeeDee had catered. Today, she was parked in the exact spot where she'd unwittingly seen the murderer running away from the scene of the crime, although she hadn't been able to identify the killer because of the darkness.

"Remind me to pick another parking spot next time," she murmured to Balto as they climbed out.

"Hey, DeeDee. Wanna see the boat?"

She turned in the direction from where Al was calling to her, and waved over to him. He was sitting in the sailboat, which was bobbing up and down on the water where Puget Sound reached the dock at the end of the garden. His Doberman Pinscher, Red, was standing guard over him, pacing up and down on the wooden boards of the dock.

"Maybe later, Al," she called back. "I just need to see Cassie for a moment about something."

Cassie was standing by the open door as DeeDee walked up to the house, and greeted DeeDee with a kiss on the cheek.

"I see what you mean about Al," DeeDee said, smiling.

"Ssh, here he comes," Cassie said.

Al's footsteps crunched the gravel on the walkway leading to the front door of the house, and a moment later he stepped into the large glass enclosed hallway beside DeeDee.

"How's the swimming going, Al?" DeeDee asked him.

"Great," he grinned. "I don't need the Swim Fin buoyancy aid any more. I had to get one specially made to fit me. Move over Michael Phelps, huh?"

"That's amazing, Al. No wonder you look so pleased with yourself." DeeDee took her cell phone out of her purse. "I know you guys have an appointment, so do you mind if I take a photo of your Alfred Mitchell painting, and I'll get out of your way?" She nodded toward the large painting hanging on the wall in the nearby great room.

Al turned to DeeDee with a frown. "Why d'ya need a photo of it?"

DeeDee stared at the painting again before she spoke. "I saw one in a Provence gallery that looked a lot like this one. It struck me as odd, that's all."

Al adjusted his ever-present sunglasses. His jaw was set in a hard line and his voice took on a menacing tone. "Ya' think there's somethin' wrong with it?"

"Probably not," DeeDee said carefully. "It's just very similar to the other one I saw. I was curious about the similarity, so I called a gallery owner in California who specializes in this type of art, and he'd like to see a photo of it. Hopefully he can clear the matter up."

Al cracked his knuckles. "If someone's gone and sold us a fake, Ima gonna kill 'em. Ya know that, don'tcha, Cassie?"

Cassie placed a hand on her husband's arm to soothe him. "Ssh, Al, let's see what DeeDee can find out first." She raised an eyebrow at DeeDee. "Thanks, DeeDee. You go right ahead, and I'll make sure Al doesn't kill anyone."

DeeDee snapped the photo and left, sensing that Al was more than a little upset about the possibility the painting might be a fake. When she got back to her car she used her cell phone to send both photos, the one she had taken in Provence along with the one hanging on the wall in the De Duco home, to Kevin at the gallery in Laguna Beach.

CHAPTER SEVEN

Simone Germain wrapped her sleek raven mane of hair into its customary knot at the back of her head and secured it with several hair pins. Her face was free of makeup, her flawless complexion needing no enhancement. Perfectly coiffed brows framed her deep-set brown eyes. Her long, straight nose gave her a look of strength that singled her out in a crowd as more than just a pretty face. She rubbed a stick of beeswax balm across her rose-colored lips and picked up her car keys and Louis Vuitton purse. Gym bag in the other hand, she sailed out of the exclusive private fitness complex without a backward glance, seemingly oblivious to the heads that turned in her direction as she made her way to the gleaming white Mercedes SUV with personalized license plates parked in front of the complex.

Dressed in a beige trench coat, cashmere sweater, and tailored pants, her lithe, tall frame had no need for high heels. Her signature shoes of choice were Roger Vivier Gommette patent leather ballerinas, and her walk-in closet at home had several rows of them in different colors. She pulled up the collar of her coat when she felt the first drops of rain, and hurried to her car, her head bowed. It was only when she was inside the car with doors locked that she found herself able to relax again.

If her eyes were the windows to her soul, the pair staring back at her in the rear-view mirror revealed a sad and lifeless existence. It wasn't that Simone didn't know she created a stir everywhere she went. She was well aware of it, but she didn't deliberately try to attract attention. If her husband had his way, he'd show her off at every opportunity that came along, just like his paintings. Simone was lonely, but being alone was preferable to being appraised like a piece of art, or treated like just another one of her husband's acquisitions. More times than she cared to count she'd wished she hadn't been so naive and desperate to get out of Saint-Victor-la-Coste when, as a teen-ager, she'd met Philippe.

He'd swept her off her feet fifteen years earlier during a visit back to his home village. "Marry me," he'd said, after a romance spanning just three weeks. Simone had accepted his proposal in a heartbeat, seizing on her chance to escape the small village where she'd grown up. Nineteen years old with no what are called life experiences, she longed to travel, see the world, and spread her wings. Her parents had refused to even let her go as far as Paris to study at one of the universities. They wanted her to stay close to them, but in the end, they had agreed to the marriage because the Germain family and hers had been close friends for years.

"Please, *madam*," Simone had begged her mother. "I have loved Philippe my whole life. You know he came back for me, just like he said he would. You must not keep us apart."

In truth, Simone had no recollection of Philippe. She had been a young girl when he'd left for the United States. When he returned, a successful businessman, the stories he told about life in America turned her head. Although she liked Philippe, and he certainly seemed enamored with her, love was never part of the equation. He did all the right things, showering her with gifts and declarations of love. For a young woman with nothing to compare it to, Simone thought what Philippe was offering her was as good as she was going to get.

After a few months of living in Seattle as a newlywed, the allure of her new life had quickly worn off. At least Philippe had been honest about his business success, and she was grateful for that. Their home was comfortable, and as the years passed and the business grew, she wanted for nothing material. However, she suspected Philippe had been less than truthful when it came to his feelings for her. She did not find his constant physical demands pleasurable, and had enjoyed both of her pregnancies for the reason that Philippe didn't find her changing body attractive when she was heavy with child. As a result, he had hardly touched her for the duration of both pregnancies, which was fine with her.

Simone closed her eyes, wishing there was some way out of the fake life in which she found herself trapped. At thirty-four, she was young enough to start a new life, but there were other considerations. She'd been over it time and again, enough that it gave her a migraine every time she tried to come up with a solution. As far as she could see, there was no way out of the prison-like marriage she'd entered into of her own free, and foolish, will.

Her cell phone rang, and the name on the screen sent a thrill of excitement coursing through her. It was Marc Germain, her husband's nephew, calling from France. "Marc, *mon chéri*," she scolded him, but her voice was sultry and unconvincing. "I've told you never to call me. We agreed a long time ago I would always call you. There must be an emergency, *oui*?"

"I consider it to be so," Marc said. "I am coming to Washington tomorrow. There are two situations I must take care of. The first is our…problem. Have you thought any more about what we discussed the last time we talked? Please, tell me you have reconsidered."

Simone let out a soft sigh. "*Mon chéri*, I have thought of nothing else. To feel your arms around me, to wake up by your side every morning, that is all I want."

Simone and Marc had grown up together, and she had never once considered him in any romantic way when they were neighbors in Saint-Victor-la Coste. It was only when he visited his uncle in Seattle as a twenty-seven-year-old artist, that a fire of lust had been ignited between Simone and him. Nine years later, it was still burning. They didn't see each other often, apart from Simone's annual trips to visit her parents in France and Marc's occasional business trips to the

United States

"You say that, but you don't act on it." Marc's tone was impatient. "The time has come to prove your love for me. I cannot live like this, knowing he is there with you, constantly touching you, when you are mine. Tell him, like you promised me you would, or I will."

Simone watched a woman walking across the parking lot who she recognized from her daughters' school. She waved at the woman and turned her attention back to Marc. "You know I've lived a lie for the last fifteen years, the whole time I've been married to Philippe, but I cannot divorce him. I come from a strong Catholic family. They and everyone else in Saint-Victor-la-Coste would never speak to me again if I divorced him. And if I were to be with you as your wife? The same would happen to you. Your family is as strong in their faith as mine."

"Simone, we are both adults," Marc said. "Our families are of no consequence. They cannot, and should not, keep us apart."

Simone laughed hollowly. "Philippe can keep me away from my children, you can be sure of that. Ava and Cecile are the only good things to have come from my marriage. My husband will fight me for custody, I'm sure of it, even if it's just to get back at me. Philippe places a lot of emphasis on appearances, and if this comes out, he won't look good. I know him. He will find a way for revenge."

"Then we will fight him in the courts," Marc pleaded. "That's what lawyers are for."

"*Non, mon chéri*, it is not to be. You know my heart belongs to you, and I know yours to me, but that will have to be enough for us. We're doomed to be star-crossed lovers."

"No." Marc said. "That may be sufficient for you, but it will not do for me. I know you can't stand my uncle. But now he's done something else, something that makes it imperative I take action." He paused. "And my action will result in our being able to finally be together."

Simone's heart was racing. She didn't like Marc's tone. He had a fiery temper, which made him a passionate lover, but also led to him acting without considering the consequences. "What is this something you speak of, Marc? Philippe has told me nothing."

Outside, the rain turned heavier and pelted against the car. A feeling of dread washed over Simone.

"Philippe sends me paintings that I sell in the gallery," Marc continued. "His prices have always been very fair, and I do well with those paintings."

"I know," Simone said. "You rely on Philippe for a large part of your income."

"Let me finish," Marc said, his voice rising. "A few days ago, he emailed me and told me I must send him seventy-five percent of the amount I receive for selling one of the paintings. When the arrangement started, we agreed I would send him only twenty-five percent of the proceeds from a sale. Those plein air paintings from Philippe take up a lot of space in my gallery, and I have many customers who want them. As you say, without his cooperation, I cannot make a living."

"Even for Philippe, that's low," Simone said. "Have you tried to reason with him? Perhaps he would agree to a lesser amount."

"What do you take me for? Stupid? Of course I have, but he's being his usual obstinate self. He told me if I don't send him the seventy-five percent, he will no longer send me any paintings to sell. End of story."

Simone stared out at the bleak rain, wishing she could see a way out of her miserable existence. She'd thought about it many times, and there was only one way that occurred to her that could permanently fix it. A life without Philippe was only going to happen if he wasn't around. As in six feet under. She shuddered, wondering how she'd become the type of woman who fantasized about murdering her husband. *Is there a type?* she thought to herself. On the true crime shows she watched on television, regular housewives killed their husbands all the time.

"What do you intend to do?" she asked, dully.

"Something I should have done a long time ago. It's better if I don't share the details with you. Just trust me. He will not have both the woman I love as well as the paintings. I may no longer be able to have the artworks, but I will have the woman I love."

There was a click at the other end of the line, and then silence. "Marc?" Simone looked at her phone. Marc had ended the call.

CHAPTER EIGHT

When Brady Saunders had finished his Master of Fine Arts in Painting degree at The University of Washington, he had dreams of becoming a famous artist. He knew he was good, and in a graduating class of six, his professors had named him the 'One to Watch.' He found himself now, four years later, churning out masterpieces just like he'd hoped he would. The irony was that the only person who had any interest in his work was Philippe Germain, who commissioned them. Brady could hardly publicize the fact that he spent his days making forgeries of expensive artworks. Even his girlfriend, Renee LaPlume, thought Brady's work was the painstaking restoration of paintings, which explained why the originals were in his studio.

He stood back and gazed at the piece he'd just finished. The original, by the renowned early 20th century California Impressionist artist, Edgar Payne, was resting on an easel next to it, and even though he'd painted the copy, he thought his version would easily pass as the original. In some ways, he thought his was better, not that it mattered. Brady often changed a brushstroke here and there, not that anyone would notice. It was his way of rebellion, making his mark on the pieces that Philippe was selling at a huge profit, while he paid Brady a much smaller share.

Brady sighed. He'd first realized he had an ability to recreate a painting when he'd taken an internship with a man called Archie

Cartwright as part of his Master's degree studies. Archie's leathery face was lined with deep crevices, the result of years of painting outdoor landscapes in Europe and California. Archie had later settled in the Northwest after getting what he called a 'real job' restoring paintings for the Seattle Art Museum.

Brady remembered the day Archie had given him a stern warning. His words were still clear in Brady's mind.

"You have a great talent," Archie said, his voice hoarse from thirty years of smoking twenty Marlboro cigarettes a day. "Don't be impatient. If fame is your ambition, it may not be fulfilled for years, if at all. Remember always to paint for love, not money. Be careful, Brady, that's my advice."

Upon hearing this admonition from his trusted mentor, Brady had a confused look on his face. "I'm not sure what you mean, Archie. I know I may not be able to sell my work until I become established, but I should be able to earn good money in restorations, thanks to your training."

Archie nodded solemnly. "Brady, you say that now, but with a gift like yours, temptation may cross your path sooner rather than later. Youth and idealism are all very well now, but when times are lean and you have bills that need to be paid, some people go to the dark side. Don't be one of those people, Brady."

"The dark side?"

That was the first time the seed was sown in Brady's mind. He knew Archie was trying to warn him to stay away from some sort of money-making scam, but Brady wanted to know exactly what it involved.

"Yes," Archie said, his eyes narrowing. "It would be possible to create fakes that would be very hard for people to tell from the original paintings, especially when using paints and canvases of the period. The only way an expert could tell the difference is if the painting was carbon dated, and even then it's difficult."

Seeing that Archie was studying his expression, Brady was careful to keep his face serious, even though a light bulb had just gone off in his head.

"I'd never resort to anything like that," Brady assured him. And he'd meant it—for a while.

But at that point in his life, Brady was tired of being poor. He was deeply in debt because of his student loans. He kept mulling over what Archie had said, shadowing him closely, and seeing how he mixed the paints for the art that had been created years ago. In fact, in some cases, it was centuries.

Archie copied the brushwork and style of the artist. He showed Brady how to research what the paints were made from at whatever time in history the painting had originated and recreate them with the same compounds. Brady continued to watch and learn from Archie, in case the day ever came when he would need to put his back-up plan into action.

Brady didn't have to wait very long. He learned soon after graduating that neither talent nor hard work was any guarantee of success. He was tired of showing his work to galleries. It was fruitless, and few, if any, gallery owners were willing to take a chance on an unknown artist with no track record. There wasn't much restoration work coming his way either, apart from a few referrals from Archie. What work he did get barely covered his rent. He wasn't sure how he was going to make money from what he'd learned from the old man, but he knew there had to be a way.

On the day he'd pushed open the door of the Germain Gallery two years earlier was the day Brady's fortunes changed. He'd been engrossed by the plein air work on display, when a Frenchman walking around the gallery struck up a conversation with him.

"It's a magnificent painting," the man had said, walking up to Brady, who was admiring a piece by Hanson Puthoff. The Frenchman extended his hand to Brady. "I'm Philippe Germain, the gallery owner. Are you a collector?"

Brady suppressed a laugh. "I wish. No, just an aspiring artist. I really like this genre. There seems to have been an explosion of the plein air movement in Seattle recently. The thing is, I think I could paint as well as these artists. Maybe I could bring in some of my pieces for you to take a look at?"

Philippe raised an eyebrow. "It's true that art collectors are very receptive right now to the Southern California plein air movement of the last century. Unfortunately, without a famous name on the bottom of the canvas, anything you bring me is worthless." He looked around to make sure that no one was listening, before continuing in a lower tone. "I kind of wish I could copy the pieces I have here and send them to my nephew's gallery in Provence, because then I could sell them twice. I sent a couple of paintings like this to him recently, and they sold immediately. It's a shame I can't get more of them, because I could get rich pretty quick."

Brady thought about it for a few moments. He stared back at the painting, Archie's warning ringing in his ears. "I can do that," he said. At that moment, he knew he'd crossed the line to the dark side.

Philippe had ushered him into his office, where they began to work out a deal. They spent the next few hours discussing the arrangement and what Philippe was willing to pay Brady to make duplicates of high value paintings. After negotiating a deal that both of them were happy with, Brady left, ready to finally make money doing what he was so good at.

He found old canvases in antique stores, at auctions, and in yard sales. It was easy to scrape off the painted surface and reapply the paint he created on the age-dated canvas or board. With meticulous precision, he copied the works Philippe gave him. He baked each painting, giving it an old appearance with cracks and all. He was careful to always use the same paint for the signature that was on the original, so if a painting was examined with a black light, the signature would not bounce, since it was painted with the same paint.

Thus began an alliance between an art dealer who was not averse to selling an original painting to a customer and telling him he couldn't have it for a week or so, because he'd promised to put it in a show or was having it cleaned prior to delivery. Philippe then gave the painting to Brady to be copied. When Brady was finished with it, and it had dried, usually within a week, Philippe let the new owner take the fake version home, which he personally bubble-wrapped. The unsuspecting buyers never questioned whether what Philippe delivered to them was the original, and it never would have occurred to them that it wasn't. Thanks to Brady, the painting was an exact copy.

Philippe then sent the original to his nephew Marc's gallery in Saint-Victor-la-Coste in France. Brady knew Marc paid Philippe twenty-five percent of what Marc sold the painting for and pocketed the rest. Marc's gallery had since developed a reputation as having excellent plein air paintings for sale at much lower prices than what one would pay for them in the United States.

Initially, Brady was happy with his cut of Philippe's profit. It was enough to make a dent in his student loans and take Renee out for dinner now and then. Getting an internship for his girlfriend Renee at Philippe's gallery had been a convenient happenstance. Brady liked spending time with her there, their shared love of art giving them something in common, although he didn't think he would have agreed for her to move in with him so quickly if he hadn't been so desperate for a roommate to pay half the rent on his apartment.

Staring at the Payne piece in his studio and the copy in front of him, Brady threw the paintbrush down, balling his hands into fists. There was no way he could paint right now, not when he was still fuming from his conversation with Philippe the previous day.

"You can't be serious?" he'd said to Philippe when the older man told him he would have to cut Brady's share of the profits. "There's no way I can accept twenty-five percent of what you're paying me right now. It's out of the question."

Philippe's reply was smooth, and Brady suspected, well-rehearsed. "It's unfortunate, but I simply can no longer pay you the generous amounts I have paid you in the past. My shipping and insurance costs have gone up considerably since we began, and I'm having to pay far more for the original paintings. *C'est la vie.*"

Brady had stared furiously at Philippe, although he managed to control his temper. He'd wanted nothing more than to wipe the smug look off Philippe's face. Brady suspected Philippe knew he would have to agree to the new arrangement, because Brady couldn't really post an ad for work as an experienced forger on the internet or in the art journals.

Brady had told Philippe he'd think it over, but if Philippe had thought that was the end of the matter, he'd underestimated Brady's anger. Brady had been seething all night, unable to think of anything else. He turned away from the paintings, and slammed one of his fists into the paint palette on the table. Paint splattered everywhere. The more of a mess he made, the angrier Brady became. He continued until his hand was bruised, and his head was about to explode.

Brady may have thought he'd escaped his childhood poverty and abusive family, but their legacy lived on in him. Not only was he now saddled with a huge debt due to his student loans, the years of mental and physical torture at the hands of a drugged-up father and alcoholic mother had left him mentally unstable and prone to violent rages. After he had a manic episode, he'd wake up with no recollection of what he'd done, other than having a bad feeling in his gut. The time he'd spent in a juvenile detention center was a distant memory, but not distant enough.

Philippe Germain will regret the day he crossed me, he thought to himself with a crooked smile. *I'll take Renee and we'll go away. She'll like that.*

A plan began to form in his mind. He'd been able to save a little money from what Philippe had paid him, and he knew there was an active market for good forgers in Europe. Even though Renee had been born in the United States, with French parentage she was fluent in the language. He could leave what was left of the student loans behind, and start again. Maybe they'd even get married. It would be perfect.

CHAPTER NINE

DeeDee glanced at the GPS screen on the dash. She was driving the van through Ravenna, a neighborhood in northeastern Seattle, on her way to Colin James' house. Although she'd spoken to Colin on the telephone before her trip to Provence to finalize the arrangements for his party, she had never been to his home. The area was named after Ravenna, Italy, and the arrow on the screen took DeeDee past Ravenna-Cowen Park and the walking route connecting Green Lake to the Burke-Gilman Trail.

It was an affluent residential area with many estate-sized homes. The arrow on the GPS screen indicated she should take the next road on the right. A call came through on the Bluetooth speaker, and she glanced at the Caller ID before answering.

"Hi, Susie. Is everything all right? I'm on my way to Colin's house right now."

"Please tell me you're not far away," Susie said. "Colin is driving me nuts. He's afraid you're going to be late, and the guests will arrive before the food is here. Talk about paranoid. He's cornered Kristen and is telling her about the temperature controls on his Meneghini refrigerator. Do you know how much those things cost?"

"The brand name rings a bell," DeeDee said, turning onto a tree-lined private street. "I'm guessing they're expensive." One thing she did know about Colin James, from another Deelish client who had referred him, was that he was mega-rich.

"Forty grand." Susie giggled. "I know because Colin told me, not once, but twice. Please hurry and save us from any more refrigerator talk with a middle-aged tech geek who has no social graces whatsoever. It's only 6:30, so the guests won't be here for a while."

"I think I'm coming up to the house now," DeeDee said, peering ahead. "There's a big glass and timber mansion down at the end, is that the one?"

"If it looks like a giant man cave, that's it. We'll come out and help you unload the van. See you in a minute." The line clicked as Susie ended the call.

DeeDee cruised into the driveway of an imposing home elevated above a sloping garden, and surrounded by tall pine trees. The exterior walls of the house were made almost entirely of glass, except for wooden columns in each of the corners of the building, making it look like a large treehouse in the middle of the pines. A metal structure resembling a space ship was perched on the roof, which DeeDee realized was the biggest satellite dish she had ever seen. *Boys and their toys*, she thought, pulling up under a covered parking area with nearby steps leading up to the house.

Susie and Kristen appeared moments later, and they helped her unload the van and carry the food up to the streamlined ultra-modern chef's kitchen. As a wine connoisseur and a member of the most exclusive club for wine aficionados in Seattle, Colin had told DeeDee he'd provide the wine, so all she had to worry about were the appetizers to go with both red and white wines. DeeDee had given Susie the recipes for the appetizers and the other dishes she wanted to serve, as well as the table set up.

"Thanks for doing all of this," she said to Susie on their third trip up the steps from the van to the kitchen. "I really appreciate you preparing everything and having the van packed up and ready for me to drive over here. I hope Colin…"

"You hope Colin what?"

Standing in the doorway of the kitchen was a tall man with graying shoulder-length hair that curled up on the collar of his navy sports coat. He was unshaven, and the rest of his outfit consisted of a crumpled designer shirt and jeans.

DeeDee set down the food containers she was carrying and walked over to him with a broad smile on her face. "I hope Colin is hungry," she said, shaking his hand. "I'm DeeDee Wilson. I'm delighted to meet you at last. Sorry if I'm a little late, but it looks like my helpers have everything under control."

Colin hesitated before returning DeeDee's smile. "I guess they do. Come with me, and I'll show you where everything is."

Colin led DeeDee through a bachelor pad that looked like it was straight out of GQ magazine. Everything about it was sleek and modern, the dark colors and styling throughout giving it a distinctive masculine edge. Large paintings hung on the bare walls, including vibrant landscapes that provided a bright contrast to the otherwise somber decor.

When they reached the other side of the house, a large deck led out onto a garden completely enclosed by trees. The outdoor furniture secured by Susie included low rattan sofas and chairs lined with sumptuous soft pillows for seating, as well as giant beanbags scattered across the grass. Fairy lights were strung around the deck and magically woven through the trees. It was still light out, but DeeDee knew as the evening grew darker, the area would sparkle.

"Your home is beautiful," DeeDee murmured. Although the style wasn't her personal taste, the setting was stunning. "Have you lived here long?"

"Long enough," Colin said. "I moved here so I can run my dogs in the nearby park. You probably saw it on your way here."

DeeDee nodded. "How many dogs do you have?"

Colin's shoulders relaxed. "Two. Cooper's a Labrador retriever and Champ's a golden retriever. They keep an old bachelor like me sane."

"I have a husky, Balto," DeeDee said. "One's plenty for me."

Colin shifted from foot to foot. "I should be getting ready. Now that you know where everything is, I'll leave you to it, if that's all right."

"I'll start getting everything plated up. Don't worry about a thing, Colin, we've got it all under control."

She watched Colin shuffle toward the glass staircase, his hands stuffed in his pockets, and then she made her way back to the kitchen to help Susie and Kristen with the appetizers.

"See what I mean about Colin?" Susie said, as she polished the silver cutlery.

"I think he's just socially awkward," DeeDee said, admiring the Meneghini refrigerator. "But I do like his taste in art and kitchen gadgets."

*****

Colin looked around the packed room, his guests laughing and drinking together like the old friends they were. He'd been anxious earlier, what with the caterer not arriving with the food until the last minute, but he had to admit, Deelish had done a superb job catering the party. The food was top-notch and complimented his wine selections perfectly. The service was friendly and efficient, without being obtrusive. The recommendation he'd received about Deelish had been a good one.

Although Colin loved entertaining, he always liked to stay on the sidelines at his own parties, wanting to make sure that everything was perfect. It was only toward the end of the evening that he allowed himself to savor the wines he'd carefully chosen, and kicked his shoes off on the grass while settling into a bean bag chair to talk with some of his former colleagues.

Colin had been one of Microsoft's first employees, a software designer. Since he'd cashed out his huge employee stock bonus and taken an early retirement, his life was one never-ending weekend. He was quite happy spending his days playing the stock market and hanging out with his dogs. Permanently single, his nights were spent alone.

Colin's friend, Ben, slumped into a bean bag next to him. "Dating anyone these days, Colin? Or are you still afraid women are only after your money? Great party, by the way."

Colin raised his glass to Ben and smiled at him ruefully. "That's rich, coming from the man in the cubicle next to me, who got married and promptly taken to the cleaners by his wife when she divorced him. Why do you think so many other Microsoft employees who made huge amounts of money when they sold their Microsoft stock and retired early like I did never married? You're the foolish exception."

Ben laughed. "Unfortunately, you and the others who retired early are all sure the only reason a woman would be interested in you is because of the large stock bonus you took when you retired from Microsoft. There's a psychologist you should go see who has a practice catering to retired Microsoft workers who never married, for the same reason you haven't."

"I'll think it over," Colin said. Out of the corner of his eye, he could see DeeDee and her helpers cleaning up. "I'll be back in a moment, I need to pay the caterer." His knees made a clicking sound as he stood up, and then he followed DeeDee through the living room toward the kitchen.

"DeeDee," he called after her. "I just want to thank you for everything."

DeeDee turned around. "You're welcome, Colin. I'm glad

everyone seems to be enjoying themselves." She held up a hand to her mouth to cover a wide yawn. "Please forgive me, I just returned from Europe and I'm still suffering from jet lag."

"In that case, let me give you a check now so you can be on your way when you're finished with the cleanup chores. My checkbook's in my office." He signaled for her to follow him down the hallway, which was lined with paintings.

"I'll wait here," DeeDee said, admiring the gallery wall, while Colin went into the office. When he came out, check in hand, he heard a gasp from DeeDee.

"What's wrong?" he asked, handing her the check.

DeeDee turned to him with a confused expression. "This is so bizarre. Two of these paintings…" she pointed to the wall, "look exactly like ones I saw recently in a gallery in Provence."

Colin shrugged. *What an annoying woman,* he thought to himself. If there were two things Colin considered himself an expert on, they were wine and art. He smiled at her condescendingly. "I'm afraid you're mistaken, DeeDee. I buy my art from a gallery with impeccable credentials, Germain Plein Air Art Gallery in Pioneer Square."

DeeDee was insistent. "I really don't think so. The strange thing is, a friend of mine also has a painting similar to one I saw in Provence as well. Would you mind if I took a photograph of these two paintings?"

Colin's eyes narrowed. "That's fine, but what for?"

"I'd like to compare them to the photos of the paintings I took while I was in Provence. Those photos are on my camera, but I don't have it with me."

"Do you think there's something wrong with them?" Colin asked in a raised tone of voice.

"No, it's just strange, that's all," DeeDee said, taking several photos of the paintings with her cell phone. "It's probably nothing." She turned back to Colin. "We'll finish cleaning up and be off, if that's all right."

Colin's reply was curt. "Excellent," he said with a nod, turning and stalking back down the hallway to the living room where some of the remaining guests had congregated. He didn't go back out to the garden to talk with Ben, because Colin couldn't get the caterer's comments out of his mind. He remembered something else that had bothered him a few weeks ago when he had guests over for dinner. His friend Jack had said he had a painting by Edgar Payne, and the signature on Colin's painting by Edgar Payne didn't look exactly like the one Jack owned.

"Maybe you've got a fake, Colin," Jack had said, taunting him.

"Or maybe you have," Colin said, right back at him.

"That, I doubt," Jack said. "I got it from the artist's family. But don't worry Col, I guess even artists have off days and the signature they use on their completed painting is slightly off from their usual signature."

Colin had laughed it off at the time, but now...alarm bells were ringing in his head.

When the catering crew and the rest of his guests had left, Colin sat down at his state-of-the-art computer and began an internet search on how to determine if a painting was a fake. He didn't notice the time creep by, until he finally crawled into bed long after midnight. By then, he was convinced from what he had learned, together with the comments from the caterer and Jack, that he'd been scammed. He'd paid a lot of money for not one, but two fakes, and Colin didn't like being taken for a fool. That was for people like Ben, not for someone careful like him.

There was nothing he could do about the situation at this time of night. He decided he'd go the gallery and talk to Philippe after his time at the coffee shop the next day. It was part of Colin's routine, from 11:00 to 2:00 every day he went to the same coffee shop, read the newspaper and talked to people, every day regulars, just like him. *Yes, that would be the sensible thing to do.*

But as the night wore on Colin tossed and turned and was unable to sleep. His attitude gradually changed from doing something sensible to doing something much stronger. Sometime in the middle of the night, he decided serious action was needed to deal with a man who would take advantage of innocent art collectors like himself. Colin was reluctant to admit that at least he could afford to get scammed. However, plenty of other innocent people could not.

I'll go to the gallery and have it out with him tomorrow, he decided. *That slimy French frog who I trusted. I'll make sure he never gets away with this. Not now, and not ever again.*

CHAPTER TEN

By the time DeeDee had returned to the Deelish kitchen on Bainbridge Island after the party, unpacked the van, and driven the last leg of her journey home, she could barely keep her eyes open. Although her body was tired, thinking about the paintings she'd seen at Colin's house was causing her mind to work overtime, and she was unable to decompress.

She took care of Balto, and then called Jake. "Hey," she said, hearing his groggy voice answer. "Did I wake you?"

"I must have fallen asleep on the sofa," Jake said. "I'm still out of whack after the change of time zones. How was the party?"

"It went well," DeeDee said. "The client, Colin James, was happy…with the catering, at least."

"I sense there's something you're not telling me," Jake said. "What's going on?"

DeeDee sighed. She explained about seeing the paintings hanging in Colin's hallway, and how he'd reacted when she told him she had seen similar ones in Provence.

"He wasn't very impressed when I voiced my concerns. I distinctly got the impression he was more than a little irritated that I'd said anything, but at least he agreed to let me take photos of them."

"I guess it's understandable," Jake said. "If someone told me they thought they'd seen several pieces of my expensive art collection somewhere else, I'd probably freak out too."

DeeDee petted Balto, who had wandered into the great room and put his paws up on her knees. "I don't think I saw them, I know I did," DeeDee said, correcting him. "I also went to Cassie's home earlier today, and looked at her Alfred Mitchell painting again. After that, I'm more certain than ever that all three of the paintings I've seen here are the same as the paintings I saw in the gallery in Provence."

She heard Jake exhale. "If it was just one, it might be a coincidence," he said. "But three? I agree this is beginning to sound sinister. Have you compared the photos you took today to the ones from the *Germain Gallerie* in Provence?"

"No, but I'll do that now. Can you hold for a few minutes?"

"Sure," Jake replied, and DeeDee set the phone down. Moving Balto's paws from her knees, she walked out into the hallway where her camera was sitting on the table. Walking back into the great room, she squinted at the shots she had taken in Marc Germain's gallery in Provence before comparing them to the more recent ones on her cell phone. The colors were the same hue, the juxtaposition just so. It was only on closer inspection that something jumped out at her.

"Jake?" Her voice was high-pitched when she got back on the phone. "I've figured it out. At first, I thought the paintings were identical, but they're not."

"What do you mean?" Jake said, sounding confused.

"The signature looks like it's off by a tiny brushstroke in all three of them. It's hardly discernible, but I'm certain of it."

Jake let out a low whistle. "Now what do we do?"

"There's something fishy going on, and I'm determined to get to the bottom of it."

"Why does that not surprise me?" Jake said.

DeeDee smiled. "Because you know I can never resist a mystery? Also, because Cassie and Al bought one of the fake paintings, I feel like they deserve an explanation. Although, judging by Al's reaction when I told him I'd seen the same Alfred Mitchell as theirs in Provence, I hope he doesn't take matters into his own hands. You know what he's like. I'd say he'd be the poster boy for a saying such as 'You can take the boy out of the Mafia, but you can't take the Mafia out of the boy.'"

"Uh-huh." Jake laughed. "Al's idea of justice is an eye for an eye, rather than waiting for the criminal justice system to slowly move its wheels."

DeeDee agreed. "I already contacted a gallery owner in Laguna Beach and sent him the photos of Cassie's painting as well as the one we saw in Provence. I haven't heard back from him yet, so I'll call him in the morning and ask if he'll take a look at Colin's paintings as well. How does that sound?"

"Sensible, for once," Jake said. "Just promise me you won't do anything else until you run it past me. As my future wife, I now have a vested interest in your safety."

"I promise," DeeDee said, a fresh wave of tiredness washing over her. "Night night."

"You too. Have a good sleep and let me know what you find out."

As soon as DeeDee's head hit the pillow, all thoughts of paintings disappeared, her mind went blank, and she instantly fell into a deep sleep. Balto, followed her upstairs as was his custom. He climbed onto the end of her bed and immediately went to sleep.

*****

The following morning DeeDee awoke refreshed, having slept well. Her head was clear, and the last of her jet lag was gone. After she had some coffee and a little breakfast, her morning walk with Balto was much more enjoyable than it had been the day before. She teased him with a stick, pretending to toss it in one direction before turning around and throwing it the other way.

Balto barked with enthusiasm, his boundless energy egging her on for more throws. When they returned to the house Balto settled outside on the grass in a sunny spot, contentedly chewing on his toy rabbit.

"I think you're tired out, Balto," DeeDee said with a grin. "If so, that's a first."

When she got inside, she picked up the phone and took it with her to the porch so she could call Kevin Morgan. She settled into the rattan seat, which creaked every time she moved. Thinking of the luxurious pillows on the outdoor seating Colin James had at his party the previous evening, she made a mental note to ask Susie where they were from, before pressing in Kevin's cell phone number.

The phone rang a few times and DeeDee thought briefly that maybe it was too early to be calling Kevin. A moment later she heard his voice.

"Hi, Kevin, this is DeeDee Wilson. I was wondering if you'd had a chance to compare the photos I sent you yesterday of my friend's painting and the one I saw in Provence?"

"Hi, DeeDee, yes I did," he said. "I'm afraid I think it's a fake."

DeeDee had a sinking feeling in the pit of her stomach. "Which one?" she asked carefully. "Do you mean my friend's painting is a fake, or the one in the gallery?"

"I'm pretty sure your friend's is the fake," Kevin confirmed. "The brushstrokes are a little off, and the signature isn't quite right. I was able to verify the one from the gallery in Provence with an exhibition catalog in my files. I believe it's genuine."

"That's what I was afraid of," DeeDee said. "Especially since I just came across two more paintings last night that I also think may be fakes." She filled Kevin in about the paintings owned by Colin James. "If I send you the photos, would you be able to have a look at those as well, please?"

Kevin confirmed that he would, and agreed to call DeeDee back after she'd sent the photos to him. She didn't have long to wait.

"I couldn't swear to it," Kevin said when he called her back half an hour later, "and I wouldn't ever put something like this in writing without personally seeing the paintings, but it's not good news. The two paintings you saw last night look like they're also fakes."

"I see." DeeDee looked out at Puget Sound, trying to make sense of what she'd just been told.

Kevin cleared his throat. "Do you mind me asking, DeeDee, what you intend to do with the information I've given you?"

"To be honest, I have no idea," DeeDee admitted. Even though her suspicions had been all but confirmed, she realized she wasn't sure what she should do now. She didn't have a plan. "All I have to go on are photos, and I'm not the owner of any of the paintings. Have you come across anything like this before, Kevin? I'm open to any advice you might give me."

"No, I haven't," Kevin said, "but I certainly will give it some thought. Unfortunately, I need to go because a customer just came in the gallery, but would you let me know when you find out something?"

"Of course," DeeDee said, getting up from her seat on the porch. "Thanks, Kevin, I really appreciate your help." She ended the call.

Balto followed her as she walked back inside and put the phone in its stand on the hallway table. She reached down to stroke his fur. "You always know when something's bothering me, don't you, Balto? I think you're a mind reader. How about if we see if Roz is free for lunch? We can go to Seattle on the ferry and meet her somewhere."

Balto wagged his tail and DeeDee smiled. "I'm not sure which is making you happier, the mention of food, or going on the ferry." Balto's tail wagged faster. DeeDee was convinced the food and ferry F words were at the top of his vocabulary.

"It's settled then," she said, lifting the phone again. "I'll call Roz and see if she's free."

She hadn't seen her sister in a while and was looking forward to telling her about Provence, as well as Jake's surprise proposal.

Another thought occurred to her. "After lunch, we can stop by the Germain Plein Air Art Gallery and see if we can learn anything. How's that for a plan, Balto?"

She turned around and looked through the open doorway, before shaking her head in amazement. Balto was already heading down the steps of the porch toward the car.

CHAPTER ELEVEN

When DeeDee and Balto arrived at the Casco Antiguo Mexican restaurant in Pioneer Square, Roz was already seated at a table in the outdoor terrace area, looking like she was thoroughly enjoying a plate of chips, salsa and guacamole. She greeted DeeDee with a messy grin before wiping her mouth with a napkin. "Sorry, Sis, I started without you. These days I need to eat every two hours without fail, with regular snacks in between."

DeeDee bent down to kiss her sister on the cheek. "Nothing new about that. Don't pretend your appetite has increased because you're pregnant, because I know better."

Roz smirked, and reached for another handful of chips.

DeeDee sat opposite Roz and looked across the table at her. She was free of makeup and there was a smattering of freckles visible across her nose, her wavy auburn curls bouncy and full. "You're radiant, Roz. I'm telling you, if the pregnancy glow could be packaged and bottled, it would sell for millions of dollars, and you could be the poster girl."

"For geriatric moms?" Roz asked, grinning. "Luckily I'm not easily offended by the medical name for an older pregnancy. Anyway, I'm doing great. I can't say the same for Clark."

The waitress brought a bowl of water for Balto, and DeeDee ordered an apple juice. "What's wrong with Clark?"

"My darling husband has sympathetic pregnancy symptoms" Roz said laughing. "He's complaining of minor weight gain, morning nausea, and disturbed sleep patterns. But he can't compete with me on the weight gain, and I've had no problems at all with the other two." She patted her growing belly for effect.

DeeDee smiled. "You're showing already, but that's twins for you. Have you thought about names for them yet?"

Roz tilted her head to the side. "Clark and I are arguing over that already. For a boy, I like Tom, in memory of our dad."

"Good choice," DeeDee murmured, glancing at the menu. "I approve."

"Clark likes Vinny, for his uncle who died a while back. Or Valentina, after his mom, for a girl."

DeeDee liked both of those names, but she sensed diplomacy was required. "They're nice, too. Why don't you each name one child? That way, you'll both be happy. What's your choice for a girl?"

Roz didn't miss a beat. "Meryl. As in Streep."

DeeDee looked up in surprise. "I'm not so keen on that for a little baby. It seems kind of…old." She watched Roz's face crumple. "I guess she'd grow into it though," she said, hastily backtracking.

She was glad to see the waitress arrive at the table to take their order.

"I'll take the plantain empanada and the house salad, please," DeeDee said, handing her menu back to the waitress.

"Vegetarian enchiladas for me," Roz said, "and the carne asada tacos." She looked over at DeeDee with a sheepish grin.

When the waitress had left, Roz leaned her elbows on the table and stared at DeeDee. "Enough about me. You're looking pretty good yourself," she said, her eyes narrowing. "There's something kind of glowy about you too. Your week away with Jake obviously agreed with you. Anything you care to share?"

DeeDee felt her cheeks flush. "Is it that obvious?"

Roz's mouth fell open, and her face lit up. "Oh. My…Gaaaaaah!!! Hurry up and tell me! Is it what I think it is?" She glanced down at Balto. "Hey fella, what's going on? Is someone going to fill me in here?"

Balto looked up for a few seconds before ignoring Roz and lazing back on the terrace, his legs stretched out in front of him. "Thanks for nothing," Roz muttered, turning back to DeeDee.

"Jake proposed," DeeDee said, her grin reaching from ear to ear. "And I said yes."

Roz reached both arms across the table to squeeze DeeDee's hands. Her eyes welled up. "I'm so happy for you," she whispered, her voice cracking. Pulling a hand away, she wiped her cheek. "And I'm so hormonal I cry at least ten times a day. Every time something pulls at my heartstrings, that's it, I'm off. It could be a song on the radio or a cute little kid walking down the street. But my big sister getting married is guaranteed to make me bawl."

DeeDee handed her a Kleenex and watched while Roz gulped back happy tears. "Tell me all about it," Roz said, sputtering with emotion. She had a faraway look in her eyes. "Don't leave anything out. Was it in a romantic restaurant by the Mediterranean, with the sun setting in the distance?"

"And violins and harp music?" DeeDee said, looking amused. "Not quite. Jake did get down on one knee, but it was on my driveway after our fifteen-hour plane trip to get home. Possibly longer, I lost track of time. There wasn't a red rose in sight."

Roz made a face. "I'll never understand you two. I'm still coming to terms with you buying him an electric drill for Christmas." She shook her head. "Then, after what was probably the most romantic holiday ever, he goes and proposes on a wet driveway. When's the big day?"

"We haven't decided. We wanted to run it past the children first, and you of course. What do you think?"

Roz threw her hands up in the air. "I think you'd be crazy not to. You know I love Jake. He's so much nicer than that first husband of yours." She scratched her head. "What was his name again?"

DeeDee raised an eyebrow at her sister. "Cute, Roz. By the way, don't ever say that in front of Mitch or Tink." Her face softened. "Lyle wasn't so bad, but thanks for giving Jake the thumbs up. It means a lot to me."

The waitress brought their food, and Roz started eating, obviously enjoying this aspect of her pregnancy.

DeeDee's empanada was delicious and sweet. The salad was made up of kale lacinata, cucumber, and carrots topped with toasted pine nuts, and a flavorful manchego cheese. She jotted the combination down in her trusty notebook which was never far from her side.

"You know you don't need my approval to get married," Roz said between bites. "Or your children's. You're a big girl, DeeDee. It's time to start thinking for yourself, and trusting your own decisions. Permission is not required."

DeeDee was quiet for a few moments. "You're right, of course. I have no doubts about getting married to Jake, but we're not in any big hurry. If it takes a while for our children to come around to the idea, we can wait for a bit rather than upset anyone."

"On the other hand, why hang around?" Roz crunched her way through a mouthful of one of her tacos. "You're not getting any younger. I think Cassie and Al had the right idea, not wasting any time. There's a lot to be said for seizing the moment. Why put off till tomorrow what you could be enjoying today?"

"I didn't know philosophy was your strong point," DeeDee said with a laugh. "Thanks for the wise words. I'll bear them in mind. I've arranged to meet Mitch and Tink this weekend, and Jake's going to run it past his daughter, Kimberley."

"Good, keep me posted." Roz stole a glance at her watch. "Do we have time for dessert?"

DeeDee gazed in amazement at Roz's two empty plates. "I'm full, but you go ahead. I'm going to visit an art gallery after this," she said casually, "would you like to come with me?"

Roz stared at her before letting out a groan.

DeeDee was alarmed. "Do you have stomach ache? If so, I'm not surprised."

"No, it's because you're acting weird," Roz said. "Every time you use that airy tone and bite the inside of your cheek like you just did, it means there's something up. What's going on?"

DeeDee sighed. She told Roz about the gallery she'd been to in Provence, and what Kevin Morgan said about the photos she'd sent him of the paintings owned by Cassie and Colin James.

When she was finished, Roz frowned. "I think you should be careful going to this gallery place. If the owner finds out you're snooping around, he might become nasty. I'd come with you, except I have a client meeting to go to that I can't cancel. Tax season may be over, but it's a new client who is being audited by the IRS. My client needs some hand-holding, since there's a lot of money at stake."

DeeDee smiled and stroked Balto, who had stood up. "It's fine, Balto and I can go. It's not far from here, and I'm sure we'll be safe in broad daylight."

"Does Jake know you're going there? Please, tell me he knows about this." Roz pushed her palms together into an upright praying position.

DeeDee paused before replying. "No, but I only thought of it a little while ago. If it makes you feel better, I'll call him and let him know."

"Fine," Roz said, signaling to the waitress. "Why don't you go and do that, while I have a chocolate fudge brownie with whipped cream. Coffee?"

DeeDee stood up and nodded. "Cappuccino." She stepped away from the table to call Jake. The call went straight to voicemail, and she left him a brief message outlining her plans.

From what she'd been able to find out about Philippe Germain, the gallery owner, DeeDee had no reason to think she was in any danger. His biography on the gallery website described him as an upstanding American citizen of French descent, married with a couple of children, and living in the affluent Seattle suburb of Bellevue with his French wife.

Nothing in his profile indicated that he was involved with a forgery ring, but DeeDee knew better than to take anything at face value. She decided she'd meet him, perhaps posing as a customer interested in buying a painting, and see what happened from there.

CHAPTER TWELVE

DeeDee strolled across Pioneer Square to the Germain Plein Air Art Gallery, where she stopped outside to admire some small paintings by Hanson Puthoff and Edgar Payne which were on display in the window. Balto was on a leash and stood next to her. Behind the front room she could see into the main gallery area, which was spacious and flooded with natural light.

The door leading into the gallery was made of thick, grainy wood with a full-height glass panel in the center, and required a hard push from DeeDee to open it. When she and Balto entered the gallery, the tinkle of a bell sounded above her head. She noticed that the floor of the gallery was covered with fake brick cobblestones. She smiled to herself at the nod to Provence that the cobblestone flooring provided, and noted that the fabric panel at the back of the gallery was just like the one in *Gallerie Germain* in Saint-Victor-la-Coste.

There was no sign of anyone inside, and DeeDee was happy to have some time to view the paintings without being disturbed. Hung against a stark white backdrop, with their only embellishment being their chunky gold frames, the thought struck her that the California plein air paintings in front of her looked sharper than the ones she'd seen in Cassie and Colin's homes. The colors were more vibrant, the lines cleaner. They looked more like the ones she'd seen in Provence.

After a while, DeeDee paused and cocked an ear toward the back of the gallery. *That's strange,* she thought, *it sounds like someone is back there, but no one has come out to greet me.* She held her breath and glanced down at Balto, who was standing rigidly at attention, his ears pricked up, and his eyes glued to the back of the gallery.

After waiting several moments longer, DeeDee called out. "Hello, is anyone there?"

The sound of heavy footsteps indicated someone was approaching, and a large, hairy hand appeared at the side of the fabric panel, tugging it open. DeeDee gripped Balto's leash, pulling him close to her. A sense of dread came over her, and she had a queasy feeling in her stomach that something bad was about to happen. She was ready to run, scream, and turn Balto onto whoever the hairy hand belonged to, if there was any sign of danger.

The drape was yanked open, and DeeDee was surprised to see a bearded man with a diamond earring. She recognized him as the man whose gallery she'd visited in Provence.

DeeDee's voice faltered, and no sound came out.

The man looked at her quizzically. "Have we met before? Your face looks familiar." The deep timbre of voice was softened by his lilting French accent, and when he smiled, his eyes lit up.

"Aren't you Marc Germain? I was in your gallery in Provence. My name is DeeDee Wilson."

Marc walked toward DeeDee and extended his hand. His handshake was hard and firm. "It's a small world. It's nice to see you again, DeeDee. It was only last week you were in my village, *non?*"

"That's right." DeeDee's heartbeat had steadied, and she loosened her grip on Balto's leash, but only slightly. "It already seems like a long time ago. What are you doing here in the States, Marc?"

Marc rubbed his beard. "I came to see my uncle, Philippe, but I can't find him. I arrived here at the gallery only minutes ago, and there's no one around."

DeeDee gestured towards the fabric panel. "Is there an office or something back there?"

Marc nodded. "Yes, there's an office and a bathroom. I just checked, and he's not in either one of those."

He was edging backwards, and DeeDee followed his lead through the fabric panel into the back area. The office door was open, and there was a half-full coffee cup sitting on a table inside the office. They walked past a small bathroom, which was also empty, before coming to a closed door. Balto growled, and DeeDee pulled him back from the door. "Where does that lead?" she asked Marc, who shrugged.

"I have no idea, but let's find out." Marc turned the handle of the door, and held it open so DeeDee could enter first. Balto made a low deep-throated growl, and DeeDee gasped. She turned to Marc, who had stepped beside her, a stony expression on his face. Before them, on the floor, lay the body of a man dressed in gray wool pants, a bright blue sweater, and wearing a cravat twisted around his neck. The toes of the man's shiny black leather shoes pointed upwards.

"Uncle Philippe," Marc mumbled, not moving.

DeeDee rushed over to Philippe, placing her index and middle fingers on the side of his neck next to his windpipe. "There's no carotid pulse," she gasped, reaching for his wrist, but there was no pulse there either. His arm was limp. She shook her head, and looked up at Marc, who stood there, unmoving. "He's dead," she whispered. "I'll call 911."

*****

The police and paramedics were on the scene within minutes.

When the Chief of Police, Dan Hewson, spotted DeeDee, he walked over to her with a frown on his face. "Ms. Wilson, we have to stop meeting like this. Every time I see you, someone's dead. And like the last time, this is going to involve a murder investigation as he was obviously stabbed to death." He took out his notebook. "Care to tell me what happened this time?"

"I met my sister for lunch earlier, and I wandered over to look at the paintings," DeeDee said, stumbling over her words.

Dan interrupted her. "Have you been to this gallery before? What was the reason for your visit?"

DeeDee hesitated. She wished Jake was there, to help steer the conversation in the right direction. Visiting a gallery wasn't a crime, and she didn't want to tell the chief about her suspicions that Philippe Germain might be involved in some sort of counterfeit art operation when she had no proof whatsoever. She suspected it wasn't the right time to be accusing a dead man of a crime on the basis of a few photographs and the opinion of a man she had met once in Laguna Beach.

"I saw some paintings I admired when I was on vacation recently in Provence, and the owner of the gallery there told me this was his uncle's gallery," she replied truthfully. She nodded toward Marc, who was being interviewed by another police officer on the other side of the room. "That's the man there. I'm interested in the plein air genre and have a background in art from working as a docent at SAM," she explained.

Dan scribbled in his notebook. "That rings a bell," he said, staring back at her. "What happened when you got here?"

DeeDee explained how she thought there was no one in the gallery until Marc had appeared, and how they'd gone into the back of the gallery and found Philippe. "That's about it," she said. "I don't know anything about the decedent, apart from having looked at the gallery's website last night before I visited."

She chewed her lip, hoping the chief would leave it at that.

He seemed satisfied. "Fine," he said, "but if you think of anything else, please let us know. By the way, how's Jake?"

DeeDee knew Jake and the chief went way back. Not only was Jake in close contact with the Seattle Police Department as part of his job as a private investigator, but Jake had told her once that he and Dan knew each other from when they were in high school and dated a couple of girls who were close friends. The double dates ended when the respective relationships with the two young girls ended, but Jake and Dan's friendship had lasted.

"He's great, thanks," DeeDee said, grateful for the reprieve.

"Give him my regards," Dan said, closing his notebook. "You have my telephone number, if there's anything else you think of to tell me. Otherwise, you're free to go."

DeeDee watched as Philippe's body was bagged up and removed, and yellow tape put up around the crime scene. She paused on the way out to wait for Marc, who was also wrapping up his police interview.

"Are you staying at your uncle's house?" DeeDee asked him. "I'm sure his wife will be glad to have your support at a time like this."

Marc smiled sadly. "Philippe didn't know I was coming. I have a room at a nearby Best Western motel. It's only a couple of blocks from here."

"I see," DeeDee said, all the while thinking it was odd he'd just show up and not let his uncle know he was coming. "I'm sorry you never got to see your uncle."

"You and me both," Marc said, giving her a glassy stare, before turning on his heel and striding away.

On the ferry ride home to Bainbridge Island, DeeDee had to restrain an excited Balto from jumping through the railings on the passenger deck, while she was on the phone to Jake filling him in on what had happened. It was one of those rare times that cell phones worked when she was on the ferry.

"I'm just glad you're all right," Jake said when she was finished. "I'll meet you at your house when you get back. How about you cook dinner, and I'll buy steaks on the way there?"

"I'd like that." The shock of finding a dead body was making DeeDee shiver, despite the mild evening. "I definitely need some comfort food after finding a corpse, and twice baked potatoes work for me. I've got all the ingredients to make them. Can you also buy the makings for a salad and some sourdough bread?"

"You got it," Jake said, ending the call.

*****

While they were eating, DeeDee and Jake discussed what they knew about Philippe Germain, and possible reasons why he was murdered.

"I'm assuming he was murdered, since the chief told you he'd been stabbed," Jake said. "But I'll be able to find out more details from my contact at the police department tomorrow."

DeeDee gave Balto a scrap of her steak. "There's a good chance Philippe was selling fake paintings to his customers," she said. "That's something I didn't mention to Dan Hewson, and I'm not sure if I should have. What do you think?"

"Let's come back to that," Jake said. "Chances are, if we know about it, the police won't be far behind. What's bothering me is why Marc would be there without telling Philippe he was coming." He gave DeeDee a knowing look.

DeeDee raised an eyebrow. "You think Marc didn't tell Philippe he was coming because he's the murderer, right?"

Jake shrugged. "It's possible."

DeeDee thought for a moment. "But he didn't know Philippe was dead. He'd already looked in the office and Philippe wasn't there. If he killed him, why would he stick around to talk to me?"

Jake stroked Balto, who was sniffing around for more steak. "Sorry, buddy, you're too late. My plate is clean." He looked back at DeeDee. "That could be a cover-up. Maybe you interrupted Marc, and he didn't have time to get away. He could have said that so you would think he wasn't the murderer."

"He'd need to have nerves of steel to pull that off," DeeDee said. "But I guess if the alternative is getting caught, it's possible."

Jake tapped the table with his finger. "There's something obvious we're missing. Maybe Colin found out his pieces were fakes, and he killed Philippe. Or...there's another more likely possibility. But I don't really want to be the one to say it."

DeeDee's eyes widened. "You mean, someone else we know and love might have done it. Like Al De Duco, by any chance?"

Balto woofed at the mention of Al's name, breaking the silence that had fallen over DeeDee and Jake.

"I'm going to ignore that option," DeeDee said after a while. "Al's not like that anymore. He doesn't just go and kill people that upset him."

Balto was twirling around, chasing his tail.

"Looks like Balto agrees," Jake said with a chuckle. "Do we know if Philippe is married, or if he has an evil ex-wife out to get him for some reason? Any disgruntled staff on the payroll?"

"According to his bio on the website he's married," DeeDee said. "But I'll see what else I can find out about his personal circumstances. Evidently he has two people on his staff, a painting restorer and a female gallery intern. I'd like to talk to his wife and those two employees. I also think we need to talk to Marc," she went on. "He told me he's staying at the Best Western near Pioneer Square."

Jake leaned closer to DeeDee, taking her hands in his. "Don't take this the wrong way, sweetheart, but why do you even need to get involved in this? The more I think about it, it's a classic case for the police to investigate. My advice is to let them take care of it and stay out of it."

DeeDee's chin wobbled. "I can't, Jake, don't you see? I was the one who discovered the discrepancies in the paintings. What if that somehow led to his death? Like it or not, I'm already involved."

Jake sighed. "In that case, count me in. While you were talking, I came up with an idea. A friend of mine is an assistant dean in the art department at the University of Washington. I'll call him right now and see if we can meet with him tomorrow. He might have some thoughts on the whole phony art thing."

He got up and stepped into the hallway, where DeeDee could hear him on the phone.

"He'll see us tomorrow afternoon," he said when he returned. He patted his leg for Balto to come over. "Why don't I take Balto for a walk, while you see what you can find out about Philippe's wife and employees?"

"That's a deal," DeeDee said, opening her laptop to begin the search.

CHAPTER THIRTEEN

"Calm down, Renee. I can hardly understand a word you're saying. What the heck is going on?"

Renee's breathless sobs, interspersed with half-formed words, left no doubt in Brady's mind that his girlfriend was really upset. She was emotional at the best of times; her gentle nature being easily bothered by things that wouldn't cause him to bat an eye. If Renee saw a stray cat in the street, she wanted to rescue it, or at the very least, give it a meal. Brady was more inclined to look the other way.

He shook his head and spoke softly into the phone, trying to soothe her. "Take a deep breath. Try again when you're ready, honey. I'm right here."

He was seated in a chair facing the window, with a view that was nothing more than the brick wall of the apartment building across the street. Sounds of traffic filtered up from street below in the rundown area where they lived. It was as far from his ideal painting location as he could imagine. When Brady had dreamed of being an artist, he had visions of working in a studio in the countryside, or preferably by the sea. The only sounds would be those of nature, except when he would play instrumental music for inspiration. The reality was far different. In his cramped apartment, with Mozart turned up to full volume, all it earned him was the anger of the neighbors, who banged on the walls or the ceiling, indicating they wanted him to turn the volume down.

At the other end of the line, Renee's wailing eventually quieted, and when she spoke again she was somewhat coherent. "Brady, I'm so glad you answered. I've never been so upset in my life. Have you heard?"

"I'm not a mind reader, Renee. What is it?"

If Renee noticed his curt tone, she let it go. "Philippe was murdered. His body was discovered this afternoon. I'm on my way to the library from class, and I just heard it on the radio. I can't believe it." She started to sob again.

A strange feeling came over Brady. His chest was tight, and it was as if something heavy was weighing him down in the chair where he was sitting. Philippe's death didn't make him as happy as he'd thought it would. It was just one of those things. He knew if he told Renee he could care less, she definitely would not appreciate it.

"I'm so sorry. I know how much you liked working for him, Renee."

Renee made a choking sound. "And I know how much you hated working for him. Don't pretend you're going to mourn his passing."

"That's unfair," Brady said, his voice steady. "My only problem with Philippe was that he wasn't supportive of my career. Philippe's numero uno priority was Philippe. Pure and simple. Not me, not you, and not his wife or family. He used everyone he knew to one degree or another. You worked for him for free, so you can hardly argue that he was your generous benefactor."

"Maybe not, but any other gallery owner would have been the same. In order to get experience, I needed to intern somewhere. Now I'm back to square one." Renee sniffed. "I guess this is going to affect both of us. I know you restored paintings for him from time to time."

Sweetheart, you have no idea how much restoration I did for him. As a matter of fact, I have a nice little savings account and I've paid off a lot of my student loans because of Philippe Germain, Brady thought.

He got up and walked across the room to where a bottle of whiskey and a shot glass sat on the table. He lifted the bottle and poured. Taking a slug, the bitter liquid caught the back of his throat and sent a warm feeling down to his chest, loosening the tightness.

"I did," Brady said, resuming the conversation, "and although I work for some other gallery owners as well, he was one of my main sources of income. Renee, I know this is a shock for both of us, and I haven't thought this through yet, but maybe it's time for us to make some changes." He swirled the liquid around in the glass, where it clung to the edges before gravity sent it trickling back down the sides.

"I can't think straight right now, Brady. I need to feel your arms around me, to make me feel safe. We can talk about it when I get home later. It's going to take a while for this to sink in, for both of us."

Brady drank the rest of the whiskey in the glass and set it down with a thump. "No," he said with urgency. "You have to listen to me, and I mean right now. I think we need to go to France for a while. There must be plenty of galleries there who could use a good restorer, and with your name, and you speaking the French language, I'm sure you wouldn't have any trouble getting a job." His mind was working overtime. "I think you even told me you have relatives in Aix-en-Provence. Maybe we could live there? I know they have a university there. You could even continue with your education. What do you say?"

Renee gasped. "Brady, there is no need to raise your voice at me like that. I'm telling you, I'm in no shape to make any decisions regarding moving to Europe or anything else. I have an exam tomorrow and the next day, and I need to study for them, which is going to be difficult considering how upset I am."

Brady swallowed. He took a deep breath before continuing, the combination of adrenalin and the whisky causing his heartbeat to race. "Of course, darling," he said. "I'm sure it will be, but you'll do just fine. Let's talk it through later. I can't wait to put my arms around you either. All I want is to be by your side, always. I love you, Renee."

"I love you too, Brady." Renee's voice was lighter. Brady knew how to wrap her around his finger, and he smiled to himself as she continued. "I'll call you when the library closes. See you tonight."

Brady stalked into the bedroom where he pulled out a suitcase from under the bed. He threw in some clothes from the stack of clean laundry Renee had left for him to put away, but which was still sitting where she'd left it in a basket on the floor. Now that he had made up his mind, he might as well start his preparations for leaving Seattle. There was no point in hanging around. This was the opportunity for a fresh start, a chance to fulfill his dreams. When Renee got home, he'd make her realize that it was the best thing for both of them. There was nothing left for them anymore in Seattle, and since Renee was madly in love with him, he was sure she would do what he wanted, after she finished her two exams.

Brady whistled to himself as he packed up the original Edgar Payne painting he'd completed. He'd take the forged copy to the gallery and leave it there before they left, so the buyer could pick it up and no questions would be asked. He assumed the police had someone there until they allowed the gallery to be reopened. He'd give it to whoever was there or leave it with the men's clothing shop next to the gallery.

Picking up his cell phone, he scrolled through the numbers on his contacts list until he came to the one he wanted. Darren Bennett was a friend of his from when they were doing their Master's degree together, and who was starting to get established as an art dealer in New York City.

"Darren? Brady Saunders here." He listened politely while Darren launched into a monologue about what he'd been doing since they last saw each other, before interrupting him. "Listen up, buddy. I've got an authentic Edgar Payne here. Going for a song. Ask no questions, and I'll tell you no lies, if you know what I mean."

He nodded at Darren's response, his foot tapping the floor at the same time, trying to wrap up the conversation. "I'd love to shoot the breeze, man, but I've got to run. Let's catch up soon. I'll ship it to you, and when you sell it, you can wire me the money, less your cut. I'm leaving town, so I'll let you know my new address. You're welcome," he said with a grin, ending the call.

Brady looked at the clock. The next two days would be busy. He needed to empty his bank account and buy euros for the trip. He also needed to make their flight reservations online using his credit card, and then present them to Renee as a *fait accompli*. Since he had no intention of coming back, he wouldn't need to pay the credit card bill or leave a forwarding address.

CHAPTER FOURTEEN

"Tell me about Scott Bayliss, your friend we're meeting," DeeDee asked Jake as they drove from the ferry terminal to the Art Department at the University of Washington. "How do you know him?"

"My ex-wife, Laura, is friends with his wife, Stacey. We used to see Scott and Stacey a lot when we were married. Unfortunately, they stayed friends with Laura rather than me. You know how it goes. I don't see much of Scott anymore. We used to go take in a Seahawks game together, or play golf now and then. As time's gone on, it's been less and less."

DeeDee smiled. "I know exactly how it goes. It's a shame people feel they have to take sides when a couple break up. Friends who I knew through my ex-husband, Lyle, suddenly dropped me like a brick after he left me. For a while I was paranoid, thinking I'd done something to offend them, or that maybe they never liked me in the first place. Then I realized it was nothing personal. In a divorce situation, people's loyalties generally lie with the person they knew first."

They parked in the parking lot, and made their way on foot on the wide pathway through the middle of the grassy Quad which was surrounded by old red brick university buildings. Inside the Quad, they were enveloped in a riot of pink, caused by the iconic eighty-year-old cherry blossom trees in full bloom.

"I forgot how amazing this place is at this time of year," DeeDee said, delighting in the picturesque scene. Students milled around on the zig-zagging pathways, and many sat on the grass. Some were reading, others chatting or simply lazing in the sunshine. "Oh, to be a student again," she said, tucking her arm through Jake's.

He smiled. "Yes. With no worries except for the cute person you have a crush on and where to go for Spring Break."

"I liked our version of Spring Break better," DeeDee said, her head filling with memories of Provence. "The lunches at *Henri's Boulangerie* and ice cream by the Mediterranean are hard to beat."

"I agree," Jake said, stopping to look around. "I think it's this one." He pointed at the building on their left. They made their way inside and followed the signs to the Art Department on the second floor.

"It's Jake Rogers and DeeDee Wilson. We're here to see Scott Bayliss." Jake said as he smiled at the secretary working in the small, cramped office. "We have an appointment to see him."

The secretary nodded. "He's expecting you. Please, take a seat in the hallway, and I'll let him know you're here.

"Thanks, Pauline," DeeDee said, reading the woman's name badge. They waited for a few minutes on an uncomfortable wooden bench.

"This reminds me of being outside the principal's office, waiting to be disciplined for something," Jake said, folding his arms.

"I wouldn't know," DeeDee retorted.

"You were always a good girl?" Jake said with a smirk.

"Maybe not," DeeDee replied, "but I just never got caught."

They were interrupted by a friendly man in his fifties wearing black jeans with a white shirt and sweater. He greeted Jake with a handshake and a slap on the back, before turning to shake DeeDee's hand. "I'm Scott," he said, "and you must be DeeDee. How you ended up with this guy, I'll never know. All I can say is, he's the lucky one in your relationship, that's for sure."

DeeDee and Jake followed Scott into his office, where art books, magazines, and papers were piled everywhere. DeeDee stood awkwardly, wondering where they were going to sit. Every available square inch of surface space in the room was covered with paperwork of some sort. The wooden bench in the hallway was beginning to look like a better option.

As if reading her mind, Scott cleared a space on a small couch by lifting a pile of books and moving them onto the floor. "Make yourselves comfortable," he said, indicating for them to sit on the couch, before scratching his head and pulling over a chair for himself. "I'd offer you some coffee, but I can't find any cups." He chuckled softly. "They're buried underneath here somewhere, and Pauline has her own mug that no one else is allowed to use. I've resorted to Starbucks three times a day. As much money as I spend there, I should probably buy some stock in that company."

DeeDee liked this man, with his sunny disposition and self-deprecating humor. She could see why Jake would get along so well with him, and felt saddened that Jake had lost touch with him as a result of his divorce.

"How can I help you guys?" Scott asked, which was their cue to tell him about the paintings in Provence, the ones that Cassie and Colin had bought from the Germain Plein Air Art Gallery, and that DeeDee had been the one who discovered Philippe's body the previous day.

"That's quite a story," Scott said when they were finished. "I heard about Philippe's death, because he was very well known in the Seattle art community. He wasn't the most popular guy on the local art scene, but he commanded a certain amount of respect because of how successful his business was."

"What do you mean, he wasn't popular?" DeeDee asked. "Why do you think that was the case?"

Scott thought for a moment. "His gallery was elitist in that he didn't support up-and-coming artists. Most gallery owners recognize the need to encourage the next generation coming up through the ranks. It's the only way to keep the art culture alive and at the same time appeal to a younger profile of buyers, so it helps everyone. Art should be inclusive, not exclusive. Philippe disregarded that philosophy in the name of profit."

"I see," DeeDee said. "That puts everything in perspective. The reason we're here is, I think the paintings we saw in Provence, and the ones at the homes of my friend Cassie and client Colin, are somehow related to Philippe's death."

"I think I know where you're going with this," Scott said with a sigh. "But I don't want to put words in your mouth. Can you tell me a little bit more about why you think that?"

"I've talked to a dealer in Laguna Beach who thinks there's something off with the paintings," DeeDee said. "He's seen both sets of photos, but he was very clear about not being able make a firm judgment unless he personally examined the paintings."

"That's what I would expect from an ethical dealer," Scott said.

Jake leaned forward and interrupted. "Ever since DeeDee told me about this, I've been thinking about it all night. Scott, by any chance do you know of anyone who would be talented enough to do that? Paint a fake that's good enough to be mistaken for the real thing?"

Scott looked away, obviously thinking about the question. Eventually he spoke up. "I have an idea. All of our students who are enrolled in the Master's of Fine Arts program have to do an internship with an art restorer at the Seattle Art Museum. He's superb. Let me call him and see if he has any thoughts about it. I'll see if I can get him on the line now."

Scott stood up and went over to his desk, where the telephone was barely visible because of the accumulation of books and papers surrounding it. He put the phone on speakerphone and dialed a number. DeeDee waited with anticipation while the phone rang.

"Hello. This is Archie," a hoarse voice said.

"Archie, it's Scott Bayliss. I've got you on speakerphone, because there's a couple of people with me who are trying to find out whether some paintings owned by people they know might be fakes. Tell me, Archie, have you ever had any students who were talented enough to create a completely fake painting based on an original?"

"Maybe," Archie said, before clearing his throat with a hacking cough. There was a long pause, and DeeDee exchanged a look with Jake, while they waited for Archie to continue.

"A couple of years ago, I had an intern who was one of the most gifted students I've ever come across," Archie said. "He was good enough that several times I let him do the restoration that was needed by the museum while I oversaw it. I've never allowed a student to do that before or since, but this young man had something special. It was like a sort of sixth sense about restoration and everything that went with it. He was intuitive about recreating whatever was necessary from a former time. Freaky, if you ask me. As if he'd been there before."

DeeDee could see Scott's face flicker with interest.

"Archie," Scott said. "Do you think the person you're referring to would be capable of copying a painting from one hundred years ago and making it look exactly like the original?"

"Sure," Archie said. "He could pretty much do that without any problem. If both paintings were closely examined side by side, the fake might be able to be spotted. Even then, in my opinion this guy was good enough to make that difficult."

Scott lifted a pen from his desk and poised it, ready to write. "Can you tell us this person's name, Archie, and where we might find him?"

"Brady Saunders," Archie said. "Last I heard, Brady was doing restoration work for galleries in the Seattle area."

Scott wrote the name on a scrap of paper. "By any chance, do you know if the Germain Plein Air Art Gallery was one of them?" he added as an afterthought.

"It's possible," Archie said. "Terrible news about Philippe, wasn't it?"

"Yes," Scott said. "Hopefully, soon someone will be able to make some sense of what happened."

With that, Scott ended the call and walked across the room to where DeeDee was sitting, and handed her the piece of paper with the name Brady Saunders written on it.

CHAPTER FIFTEEN

DeeDee climbed back into the car. "Do we have time to visit Simone Germain?" she asked, as she secured her seatbelt with a click. Jake had mentioned that his assistant, Rob, had texted him the Germain family's address that morning after DeeDee had asked if he could get it for her. The previous evening she'd spent some time online researching Philippe, and had uncovered some interesting information.

"Sure," Jake said, driving out of the university campus and heading in the direction of Bellevue. "Rob and I are working on a couple of cases and I need to meet up with him later, but we have the rest of the afternoon. We might as well make a day of it."

In Bellevue, they easily found the Germain home which was in the Beaux Arts Village located on the shores of Lake Washington. As Jake drove slowly past the house, DeeDee craned her neck to catch a glimpse of the picture-perfect two-story home with a double garage. The gates were open, and the residence was tucked away just out of view from the street, down a winding brick driveway surrounded by a wooded garden. There was space for a couple of cars out front, and there was a circular driveway in the front of the house.

"Wow," Jake said, as they passed one beautiful home after another, all on the shores of the lake. "Just wow. I've never been to this area before. It's hard to believe somewhere this close to Seattle has its own private beach in a wooded enclave."

"I know," DeeDee said. "It's a little world of its own. Who wouldn't love to live in an exclusive community with a small town feel, right on the edge of the city?"

Jake parked on a tree-lined street a few houses up from the lake. They made their way back to the Germain home on foot, not passing any other pedestrians along the way, although several cars went by, all luxury models.

At the Germain house there was a silver Toyota Prius that appeared to be a rental car parked in the driveway along with a shiny white Mercedes SUV. They walked up a pathway leading to the house and climbed the steps that led to a wraparound porch and the front door.

Before DeeDee could ring the doorbell, Jake motioned to stop her. The sound of raised voices was coming from inside the house, a dialogue of rapid-fire French.

DeeDee strained to hear, but could only make out a few words.

"Can you understand what's being said?" Jake asked in a low voice.

DeeDee shrugged, then pointed to an open window a few steps away from the door. They quietly stepped next to the window, where the heated exchange came through loud and clear.

Jake looked at DeeDee questioningly, and raised his hands for some indication about what the people inside were talking about, but she just cocked her ear and concentrated on trying to translate. Most of the words she could understand, and she was able to piece together the parts she didn't by the context of the rest of the conversation.

After listening for several minutes, DeeDee was startled by the front door being flung open. She watched Marc Germain storm out of the house, muttering under his breath. He did not look in the direction of where they were standing on the porch which was several steps away from the door, and strode down the steps to the rental car.

He was almost immediately followed outside by a woman DeeDee assumed was Simone Germain. Through various online clippings and interviews DeeDee had read on the internet the evening before, she had learned Simone was twenty years younger than her deceased husband. She had married him when he was on a trip in Provence to visit his family who lived in the small village of Saint-Victor-la-Coste, the same village where DeeDee and Jake had vacationed the previous week.

The way Philippe portrayed the story in the snippets she'd read of how he met and married his wife, made it sound terribly romantic. Simone, seemingly trapped in small village life, was desperate to get away and do something more meaningful, but her tight-knit family refused to let her leave to study in Paris. They wanted her to stay close to them, and she did, until the dashing Philippe came back to the village from the United States, and like a knight in shining armor, rescued her from her boring life in the village. Not only had he swept her off her feet, but he had swept her away from Saint-Victor-la-Coste to the United States, and given her the happily-ever-after dream she'd always wanted.

Simone was beautiful in the flesh, and DeeDee thought the online photos she'd seen of her hadn't done her justice. Dressed in a classic beige linen sweater, cropped Armani pants, and leather ballet pumps, which DeeDee recognized as being eye-wateringly expensive, the Frenchwoman was the epitome of chic. Her presence on the porch was accompanied by a waft of floral scent that screamed sexy and sophisticated all at once. DeeDee saw that Jake was also staring at Simone, and was happy to notice that there was no sign of attraction in his gaze, just a curious fascination with this model-like creature.

DeeDee spoke up. "Mrs. Germain, may we talk to you for a moment?"

Simone was startled by the sound of DeeDee's voice. She first looked at DeeDee and then at Jake, creases appearing on her otherwise flawless, milky forehead. Surprise and bewilderment were etched across her face, but what struck DeeDee most of all was the pain in her eyes.

Simone turned to where Marc was backing rapidly out of the driveway, tires screeching, before addressing DeeDee's request with a weary shake of her head. "Can it wait for another time?" she asked. Her voice was soft, and a tear trickled down her cheek. "This really is not a good time for me. You see, my husband was murdered yesterday, and there are many things I must do."

DeeDee stepped forward. "Mrs. Germain, I'm DeeDee Wilson, the person who discovered your husband's body. I've come to express my condolences and see if you can think of any reason why your husband was murdered. I'm sorry I don't speak French, but it's obvious you speak English well."

DeeDee's cheeks flushed. Out of the corner of her eye she could see Jake looking at her with a puzzled expression. She knew he'd understand later why she felt it necessary to lie about not speaking French, and hoped he'd play along. To his credit, Jake stuffed his hands in his coat pockets and stayed silent.

"In that case, please come into the house," Simone said, leading the way.

DeeDee and Jake followed her into a home with paintings on every wall. It was clear either Philippe or Simone loved orchids, because they were everywhere, in every color, and in every size. The furniture and everything else were all in neutral shades, providing a monochromatic backdrop for the bursts of color from the paintings and the vibrant orchids.

"Please, have a seat," Simone said, gesturing towards a large cream-colored sofa in the living room. DeeDee noticed a Hermes purse flung casually on a side table, which she noted probably cost more than DeeDee's car parked down the street.

"Again, we're sorry to bother you," DeeDee said when they were seated. "This is Jake Rogers, a private investigator. I never met your husband, but Jake and I were at the *Gallerie Germain* in Provence last week and met your husband's nephew, Marc. As a matter of fact, Marc was with me when I discovered Philippe's body." She paused, studying Simone's body language. "I think that was him who just left?"

Simone shifted in her seat, and fidgeted with her hands. "Yes, we are trying to make arrangements regarding what to do with my husband's body and his business. His family is still in France, but trying to transport the body for burial in another country could be problematic. As far as the gallery's future, I don't know."

DeeDee nodded. *That's not what you were talking about with Marc, Madame, but I'll play along,* she thought.

"I'm certain there are many decisions to make," Jake said. "Going back to DeeDee's original question, can you think of anyone who would want to murder your husband? Did he ever mention employees who were unhappy, or even disgruntled customers by any chance?"

"No," Simone said. "He only had two people who worked for him. His intern, Renee, had been with him for over a year and from what Philippe told me, she was very happy with her job. He had a restorer who worked for him from time to time, Brady Saunders, but I never heard of any problems there. In fact, Brady was the one who recommended Renee to Philippe. As far as customers, I don't know. I didn't work at the gallery or visit there often, but there were no issues I was aware of."

"When I was at the gallery in Provence," DeeDee said carefully, "Marc mentioned that Philippe would buy California plein air paintings in the United States and send them to Marc to sell at his gallery in France because that style did so well over there."

DeeDee watched Simone's eyes quickly dart away. Simone swallowed and turned back to DeeDee, not catching her eye. "That's true, but I know nothing of the details. Now if you'll excuse me, I really do have things I need to do."

Simone stood up and started walking in towards the hallway. DeeDee and Jake took that as their cue to leave. Simone held the door open with a vacant stare while they exited, both of them thanking her for seeing them. They were hardly down the steps when the door shut behind them with a bang.

When they were out of the driveway and walking back down the street toward their car, Jake turned to DeeDee. "Are you going to tell me what all the shouting was about when we arrived? What were they saying?"

"Nothing like what she told us. Marc told her they could finally be together, and she asked if the thing he said he was going to do when he came to the United States was kill Philippe. Marc was protesting his innocence, and said they needed to make plans to go back to France before someone else thought he was the murderer. Then he threw it back in her face by saying he had thought she would be glad Philippe was dead, since he knew she never loved him. They argued about that for a bit. Mostly, Marc was pleading with her, asking if she was ready to go with him or not."

When they arrived at the car, Jake held the door open for DeeDee. "I thought you said Simone and Philippe have a couple of children. Do you really think Simone would just up and leave them to be with Marc?"

"I'm just getting to that," DeeDee said, as Jake got in and they drove off. "Simone did talk about them. Her exact words were, 'What about the girls? They will never forgive me if they find out what I have done.' Then she said she needed a little time to think about it and make plans. That's when Marc stormed out."

Jake rubbed his chin. "Well, in that case, if they were having a love affair, that could be Marc's motive for the murder. Kill his uncle and get his wife."

"That's true, but it doesn't solve the problem of the paintings. And what did Simone mean when she said her children would never forgive her for what she had done? Maybe she wasn't talking about the affair, maybe she meant she had killed their father."

"I agree. We'll just have to keep thinking about it until we find the right answer, but for now, it's getting late and if we don't get to the ferry terminal pretty soon, we're going to be out of luck. The commuters will all beat us to it."

On the ferry ride to Bainbridge Island they stood on the passenger deck and talked about what to do next. Jake put an arm around DeeDee's shoulders, and she leaned her head on him, gazing out over the Sound. "I need to get ready for a few catering events I have coming up, but would you be able to join me in Seattle tomorrow afternoon?"

"I should be able to," Jake said, leaning down to kiss the side of her forehead. "Rob and I have some work to do that will take most of this evening and tomorrow morning, and then I'm free. What do you have in mind?"

"When I spoke to Colin James about his party requirements before we went away, I remember he asked if I could meet him at his usual coffee shop." DeeDee thought for a few seconds, trying to remember the name. "The Daily Grind, that's the one. He told me he goes there every day from 11:00 in the morning to 2:00 in the afternoon. As it happened, Susie ended up meeting him instead of me. I thought I could try and find out if Colin was there yesterday when Philippe was murdered. Depending on what time he left The Daily Grind, that could be his alibi and it would eliminate him as one of the suspects."

"Good idea," Jake said, as the ferry pulled up to the Bainbridge Island terminal. "I also suggest we find out where Renee lives and pay her a visit, and maybe Brady as well. I'll have Rob get addresses for them."

"Thanks, Jake," DeeDee said, reaching for his hand and giving it a gentle squeeze. "Looks like tomorrow's going to be another busy day."

CHAPTER SIXTEEN

The next morning, after their usual walk on the beach, Balto made a whining sound when DeeDee started getting ready to go out again. He watched as she pulled on her coat, and he hung his head at the rattle of her keys when she picked them up from the hallway table.

She reached down to rub his fur. "I'm sorry, big guy, I can't take you with me today. I have to go to work."

Balto shook DeeDee off, and walked over to the front door, where he lay down blocking her path.

"It's like that, is it?" she said, laughing. She was on her way to see Susie at the Deelish combination office and kitchen to do some prep work and planning for several upcoming events, and there was no place for a dog there. "I don't like how you go off in a huff every time I have to do something that doesn't involve you. And you can quit giving me that mean stare while you're at it, it's not working."

Balto made a sad face, and lay his head on the floor.

"I give up," DeeDee said, turning to go out the back way. She smiled to herself as she heard Balto get up and follow her. It was the same routine they often played out. Once outside, she locked the back door, settled him in the fenced area of the yard, and made sure he had enough water to last the rest of the day.

When she arrived at Deelish, Susie was already there, making a list of supplies they needed to order for the two events they were catering the following week. Susie had also neatly stacked the receipts for the purchases she had made for Colin James' party, and entered them into the red hardback notebook they kept for the accountant.

"I don't know what I'd do without you, Susie," DeeDee said as she pulled out a high stool and sat beside her assistant at the counter. "I'd like to give you a raise. Deelish has reached the point where I can charge enough that I'm happy with the amount of work coming in, and I don't really want to take on many new clients. I know you're hoping to open your own catering business at some point, but I don't want to lose you."

"I won't say no to a raise," Susie said, the gap between her front teeth flashing when she smiled. "And don't worry, I'm not yet at the point of starting up for myself. I like working here, as well as my other two jobs. But if you do ever have any extra work I'd be happy to take it on separately, with your approval, of course."

"Let me think it over," DeeDee said. Susie was a hard worker, and when she wasn't helping DeeDee at Deelish, she knew Susie picked up waitressing shifts at a coffee shop in Bainbridge Island as well as at a high-end restaurant in Seattle. "I'm sure we can work something out."

She spent the next couple of hours with Susie working on planning menus, finalizing the online shopping order, and agreeing what items Susie would pick up fresh from the farmer's market before their next event, a Bar Mitzvah in an outdoor tent at a home on Mercer Island.

There was a knock on the door a little after noon, and Jake entered, holding three Starbucks coffees. "My hero," DeeDee said, faking a swoon, as he passed a cup to them.

"Are you ready to catch the ferry to Seattle?" Jake asked, his blue eyes dancing.

"We were just finishing up," DeeDee said.

Susie nodded. "You guys go on, and I'll lock up here. I want to test a recipe for cookie bars before I leave."

Jake hesitated. "Maybe we should stay, in that case."

DeeDee pushed him toward the door, with a backward wink at Susie. "Thanks, Susie, I'll talk to you later."

"Do you need to go home first to see to Balto?" Jake asked as they walked out to his jeep. "We'll go in my car, and I'll drop you back here to pick yours up later."

"No, I've taken care of him for the day. Although he's developing quite an attitude. If I was a pushy dog-mom, I'd be trying to get movie auditions for him. As it is, he's a diva enough already."

Jake opened his mouth to speak, and she gave him a warning look, knowing that he was about to give her the benefit of his doggie wisdom. "And no, I don't need your advice, thank you very much. I'm perfectly capable of dealing with Balto's quirks by myself."

"As you like," Jake murmured, getting into the car. "As you like."

They took the ferry to Seattle and retraced their route back to the University of Washington, where they had been the day before.

"Rob said Renee lives with Brady Saunders," Jake explained, as they walked through the spent cherry blossoms scattered on the ground. "He was able to get her class schedule and she had an exam this morning, but she should be free this afternoon. Usually, if she's not in class she can be found in the library or at the Germain Plein Air Art Gallery. I took a guess she's more likely to be on campus, since I don't know if the gallery has re-opened after the murder."

They asked a passing student the directions to the library, and found it after a five-minute stroll through the Quad. At the reception desk, DeeDee explained that they needed to urgently speak with

Renee LaPlume concerning a personal matter. "Would you be able to page her to see if she is here, please?"

The receptionist snarled back at her. "Nope. We don't do that. I'm not a concierge, I just check the books in and out and collect the fines."

DeeDee thought there were scanning machines that did that, but she didn't want to argue with the snarly librarian with badly drawn-on eyebrows.

Jake took some cash out of his pocket and peeled off a hundred-dollar bill.

"I know you're not a concierge," he said politely, pushing the bill across the counter. "But would this help?"

The woman eyed the bill under Jake's hand, and promptly made an announcement on the public address system for Renee La Plume to come to the reception desk. "Take a seat over there," she barked, nodding to some nearby chairs, while Jake lifted his hand so she could take the money.

"Thank you," Jake said, giving her his best fake grin before steering DeeDee toward the seating area.

The young woman who appeared at the reception desk several minutes later was of medium build and dressed in a light green sweater dress with knee-high boots. She wore a cheap necklace with pasted-on colored glass gemstones, and her straight, shoulder length mousy hair was tucked behind her ears. The librarian pointed to where DeeDee and Jake were waiting, and scowled before going back to her work.

DeeDee, seeing the young woman's worried look, stood and approached her.

"Renee?" she said softly. The woman nodded. "I'm DeeDee Wilson. I was at the gallery when Philippe's body was found." She watched Renee's chin wobble, and had an urge to comfort her. "Would you mind if my friend and I talk to you for a few minutes? I promise we won't take up much of your time."

"Fine," Renee said quietly. "I need to leave soon anyway. I've had exams the past couple of days, but now they're over and my boyfriend and I are taking a trip." She followed DeeDee over to where Jake was waiting.

"This is Jake Rogers, a private investigator," DeeDee explained when they were seated. "We are both very sorry about what happened to Philippe."

"Thank you," Renee said. "It's been a big shock for me. I saw him that morning, before…" She looked away, and sniffed.

"It must be very difficult for you," DeeDee went on. "The reason I've developed an interest in the case is because of some paintings I saw in Provence, and ones I've seen here in Seattle that were purchased at the gallery."

Renee stared at DeeDee, her face not registering anything when DeeDee referred to the paintings she'd seen in Provence.

"Jake and I know the chief of police," DeeDee continued, "and thought we'd see if we could find out something that might help catch whoever is responsible for Philippe's death."

"I've been thinking about this ever since I heard he was murdered," Renee said, wiping her nose with the back of her hand. "I can't think of anyone who would have a reason to murder him. He was at work most of the time. I spend a lot of time at the gallery, and he did not seem to have any enemies." Her eyes shone as she spoke of him. "I think Philippe was a wonderful man, and I admired him greatly."

"I see," DeeDee said, wondering if Renee's admiration for her former boss had been reciprocated in any physical way by Philippe.

"We heard Philippe only had two people who worked for him," Jake said, "you and the man who did some restoration work on paintings at the gallery. Do you know your co-worker well?"

A flush of pink spread across Renee's cheeks. "Brady? Yes, we've been seeing each other for some time. I met him when I was starting the art program at the university and Brady was finishing his Master's degree. It was Brady who introduced me to Philippe when I was looking for some work experience."

DeeDee gave Renee a smile of encouragement, and the young woman continued. "I was a little older than most of the other students when I started college, but I had to work when I finished high school and save enough money to go to college. My parents didn't think college was a priority for a woman. They had spent their money helping my brother get a college degree." She shrugged. "That's just how it was in our house."

DeeDee wanted to know more about Brady's restoration work. "Does Brady paint on his own or just restore paintings?" she inquired.

"As far as I know, he just restores paintings," Renee said. "He uses the second bedroom in our apartment for his studio. I've tried to encourage him to paint his own stuff, but he seems to have given up. He doesn't like me going in there, so I respect his privacy." She chewed on her lower lip. "Brady's a brilliant restorer, and it paid him very well. He told me once it was pretty much impossible for an artist just starting out to sell his works, and he'd decided to go the route of restoration instead. Now that his income has disappeared overnight, Brady wants us to leave Seattle. He thinks we would have much better opportunities somewhere else."

"Do you know of any customers who were unhappy about anything?" Jake asked.

Renee thought for a while before shaking her head. "No, because Philippe had superb pieces and the customers were always happy with what they bought. The works in the gallery were so well thought of they were often loaned out to be in other shows. They were so popular that when someone bought a piece from the gallery, it often was a little while before the customer could take home the painting they had bought. Even so, the customers didn't mind because they were so happy to get it."

"When someone bought a painting," DeeDee said, "did Philippe give the customer information about the history of the piece as part of the purchase? I remember when I bought one years ago, the gallery owner gave me a printout of everything about the painting."

Renee nodded her head vigorously. "Yes, of course. Philippe did the same. When the customer picked up the painting, they were always pre-wrapped in bubble wrap, and he'd give them a photo of it as well as the information in a large envelope."

"That's really helpful, thanks, Renee." DeeDee looked over at Jake. "I don't think I have any more questions, do you, Jake?"

"I can't think of anything else either." He turned to Renee with a smile. "Thanks for your time, Renee. We won't keep you any longer."

Renee walked them to the door of the library, Jake giving the grumpy receptionist a cheery wave on the way past.

"Renee looked deep in thought as we were leaving," DeeDee commented outside. "Do you think she did it?"

"I doubt it," Jake said, "But I'd still be interested in meeting this Brady Saunders guy. I think I've figured out what kind of a scam Philippe was running, though."

"What do you mean?"

They got into the car. "What if," Jake said, as he backed out of the parking space, "the painting the customer got was not the one they bought, but a very well-done copy of it? The customer thought it was the same painting because of the photo and all the official information that came with it. When they got it home and took the bubble wrap off, I'm betting the buyer would probably never notice the small little details that might be different from the original. Don't forget, by that point it's probably been a couple of weeks since they saw the original. Maybe that's why he always bubble wrapped the painting for the customer, so they didn't look at it too closely when they picked it up from the gallery."

DeeDee stared out the window. "It's plausible," she said with a sigh. "But since Philippe is dead, it might just be impossible to prove your theory."

*****

At The Daily Grind coffee shop, Jake ordered a grilled pancetta mac and cheese panini and a coffee.

"I'll have a *pain au chocolat*," DeeDee said, nostalgically thinking of Provence, "and a raspberry tea."

They sat at a table by the window. The coffee shop was small, and a quick glance around at the handful of wooden tables told DeeDee it seated no more than forty people when it was full. Even though it was early afternoon, there was still a line for takeout, which was where DeeDee presumed the business made most of its money.

"Do you ever think about opening a little place like this?" Jake asked, waving his hand across DeeDee's line of vision to get her attention.

"Sometimes," she admitted. "And then I think I'd be chained to it all the time, not to mention the employee dramas to deal with if someone didn't show up for their shift. And the overhead to run a place like this is much higher. I don't think I'll be opening a chain of Deelish cafe's any time soon. This place is nice, though. I like the quirky touches like the different blooms on every table and the bunched-up milk bottle hanging lights."

The waitress brought their order. "Thanks," Jake said. He casually added, "I thought Colin might be here. He's a friend of mine. Has he been in the last couple of days?"

"Sure has. You've just missed him. Every day you could set your clock by that guy. Comes in precisely at 11:00 in the morning and stays until 2:00 in the afternoon. He told me once he works out in the morning."

"Yeah, that's right," Jake said. "I should follow his example and visit the gym more often myself."

The waitress eyed Jake up and down. "You look all right to me. Anyway, I've been on the day shift the last three days, so I can guarantee you he was here every one of them. Come back tomorrow morning around 11:00. I'm sure he'll be here then, too. He loves to talk to people and read the newspapers and magazines about the stock market. In fact, he's such a good customer we get his order ready just before he comes in. To my knowledge, he hasn't missed a day in, oh, I don't know how long."

"Thanks for the information," Jake said. "Guess I'll just have to get here earlier next time."

The waitress walked away, leaving DeeDee to tease Jake about his hot gym body.

"Finished?" he asked DeeDee, after wolfing down his panini.

"Yep. I think I'll save the *pain au chocolat* for when I'm in France, all the same. *Henri's Boulangerie* has spoiled me for life."

As they were walking away, DeeDee voiced what they both had been thinking. "It sounds like Colin's in the clear. When the coroner was examining Philippe's body, I overheard him tell the chief that Philippe had been dead no longer than an hour. I discovered his body about 1:30 p.m., so there's no way Colin could have done it. He was at The Daily Grind when Philippe was murdered."

"I agree," Jake said. "I think we need to go see Brady Saunders. You up for that?"

"Yes. I'm beginning to think it was Marc or him. Simone may not have been in love with her husband, but she didn't strike me as a ruthless killer. Plus, neither Renee or Simone look strong enough to have dragged Philippe's body into the storeroom where he was found. Unless there's a lot we don't know, we've pretty much run through the known characters or should I say suspects."

CHAPTER SEVENTEEN

As Jake was parking down the street from the apartment where Brady and Renee lived, DeeDee saw Renee hurrying up the sidewalk.

"Oh my goodness, look the other way," she said to Jake sharply. "Renee is walking right towards us." DeeDee pretended to look for something on the floor of the jeep, while Jake turned his face to the street, so Renee wouldn't recognize them.

"She's gone, so you can stop eating the carpet," Jake said with a laugh a few seconds later.

DeeDee half-laughed, half-groaned. "Do you think she saw us?"

"No," Jake said, "she looked like she had a lot on her mind. Let's wait a few more minutes to make sure the coast is clear."

DeeDee scrolled through her phone while Jake checked Renee's progress in the rear-view mirror.

"I'm meeting Tink and Mitch for lunch tomorrow," DeeDee said, glancing over at Jake. "To tell them about our news."

"Oh yes, I'd forgotten about that," Jake joked. "Our wedding. Let me know the date, and I'll make sure I'm free."

DeeDee lightly tapped him on the arm with her phone. "Very funny. When are you going to speak to Kimberly about it?"

"As you know, my eighteen-year-old daughter can be quite elusive. Seeing her old man isn't high on her priority list, particularly now that she has a boyfriend and can drive. However, I have a plan."

"What's that?" DeeDee asked with a frown.

"I said I'd pay for her prom dress and other expenses. That way, she needs to meet me in person, so I can hand over the money."

"Good thinking," DeeDee said, her face relaxing. "Although I'm sure that's going to cost you a lot. You're such a big softie that if it came to a thousand dollars, you'd pay it."

It was Jake's turn to frown. "Really? You think it could be that much?"

DeeDee raised an eyebrow. "Oh, Jake. You really have no idea. If you get away with half of that amount, you'll be lucky. Girls these days go all out on the prom. Designer dress, hair, makeup, spray tan, limousine, the full works."

"She can forget the limo, I'll offer to give her a ride myself," Jake said, open-mouthed. "Just kidding. I have a feeling that idea would fall flat."

"At least you have something right," DeeDee said.

He checked his mirror again. "Renee just went into the apartment building," he announced. "It should be safe to follow her now. Are you ready?"

They got out of the car and headed in the same direction as Renee, entering the apartment building and taking the stairs to the second floor. When they got there, DeeDee cautiously opened the door from the stairwell to make sure Renee wasn't in the hallway.

"It's clear," she whispered. She clutched Jake's hand and they walked the rest of the way down the corridor without speaking, stopping in front of the apartment number Rob had given to Jake.

They could hear Renee's voice coming from inside the apartment. "Brady, what is this and why is it still here?" she yelled.

DeeDee noticed that Jake had taken what looked like a small tape recorder from his pocket and pressed a button on it. Her attention was drawn back to Renee's voice.

"I thought you took that painting back to the gallery yesterday. You said you'd finished restoring it and wanted to leave it at the gallery, even though it was still yellow-taped, to make sure the customer would get it on time, and it would be there when the gallery re-opened. Did you keep it because you haven't been paid yet? There's no need to worry about that. I'm sure Simone will honor the payroll."

"I can explain." A man, who DeeDee assumed was Brady Saunders, was speaking. "It's not what you think. And I told you before about coming into my studio. It's an invasion of privacy."

"It's not an invasion of privacy when I pay half the rent," Renee pointed out sharply. "I came back because I was worried about you. I had a conversation with a couple of people today who were asking me about your work. I thought if I could encourage you to take up your own work again, it would make you happier. You seem so angry lately."

"What people? Why were they asking about me?"

"People investigating Philippe's death, that's who. What's gotten into you these days? You know how excited Mrs. Jennings was when her husband bought this painting as a gift for their anniversary, and you said you didn't want her to be disappointed. I saw you walk out the door with it yesterday, wrapped in bubble wrap under your arm, to take it back to the gallery. Did you wait until I was gone, and come back with it because you couldn't even be bothered to make the trip?

Or did the yellow tape stop you?"

"No!" Brady was shouting now. "I did bring it back. Please, let me explain."

"It better be good," Renee said. "Because unless I'm seeing things, the exact same painting is still sitting on the table in front of me, half-wrapped in bubble wrap with a shipping label beside it. Tell me I'm mistaken, and you haven't stolen the painting and are not about to send it off somewhere to be sold. If I hadn't come back when I did, maybe I never would have known."

"I've been wanting to show you what I've been doing for a long time, but I was afraid you might let Philippe know that I'd told you, and he'd sworn me to secrecy." Brady sounded triumphant. "Now it doesn't matter. Don't you see what I've done, Renee? I'm truly an artist. Philippe has been giving me paintings once they've sold at the gallery, and I've been copying them. Then Philippe would give my painting to the customer and send the original paintings to his nephew's gallery in France to be sold again. Do you know how talented someone has to be to do something like that? To have fooled so many people, for so long?"

It was quiet for a moment until Renee spoke up again. "You're insane, Brady. You and Philippe knowingly cheated customers who trusted him. They believed they were getting authentic paintings and instead, Philippe was passing off your fakes as originals. I'm disgusted with both of you. Brady, selling something as an original when it's not is against the law. I'm no lawyer, but even I know that. What were you thinking of?"

"You're right," Brady said, "and that's why we're going to France. I don't want anyone to find out what I've been doing, but I know it will be easy for me to get work over there. I've made our plane reservations, and we're going to leave tonight. I knew how important those exams were to you, so I waited until you'd finished. I've even bought new clothes for you, so you'll have everything you'll need. I wanted to surprise you, Renee."

"You've surprised me all right, Brady," Renee said, her voice choking up. "I said I'd consider moving away from Seattle, but not like this. I won't be going to France with you, or anywhere else for that matter. I could never be with someone who defrauds people. I could never trust you again."

Brady laughed, a hollow menacing sound that sent a shiver down DeeDee's spine. "Well, what about someone who committed the perfect crime? You think anyone will ever figure out that I'm the one who killed Philippe? I mean, where's the motive? No one knows that he was going to cut my share to peanuts. No, I'm just someone who did restorations for his gallery from time to time. He always paid me in cash for them, so there's no trail. Now come on, we need to get going. Traffic can be tricky this time of day, and SeaTac is always busy. I'll get our suitcases. They're in the bedroom."

"You really are crazy. I'm not going anywhere with you. I thought I loved you, but the person I loved was the man I thought you were, not the real you. You're a fake, Brady, just like your crummy paintings. Do what you like, but I'm leaving. Alone."

DeeDee heard footsteps walking across the floor, then a scream. "Get off me," Renee called out.

When Brady spoke again his tone was threatening. "I'm sorry, Renee, no dice. You've given me no choice. We're going to take a little walk into the bathroom. If you scream again when I put the knife in you, no one will hear it when the toilet's flushing and the water's running."

DeeDee's heart was pounding as Jake let go of her hand and pulled out his gun. He kicked the door until it burst open on the fourth kick and yelled, "Drop the knife, Brady, or I'll shoot."

DeeDee gasped from her vantage point in the doorway. Brady, yielding a large kitchen carving knife, was pushing Renee into a room at the end of the dimly lit hallway. When Jake entered, Brady whirled around and lunged toward Jake, murder in his eyes. Renee turned and stood frozen in horror while Jake took aim and fired his gun. When

Brady crumpled to the floor, DeeDee heard the click of the lock on the bathroom door, behind which Renee had suddenly disappeared. Brady was screaming in pain, Jake's bullet having hit him in the shoulder.

"DeeDee, call 911," Jake instructed her. "I don't want to turn away from him."

Her hands trembling, DeeDee made the call. When she'd finished giving the details to the police dispatcher, Jake called out in a loud voice. "Renee, it's all right. You can come out of the bathroom now. Unlock the door. Everything's okay. I have Brady covered, and the police are on their way. I can hear the sirens."

A cowering Renee walked out of the bathroom and into DeeDee's comforting arms. The two women waited in the living room for the police while Jake held his gun on Brady who was laying on the floor of the hallway.

"Please, don't make me look at him," Renee said, shivering on the sofa. "I never want to see Brady again." DeeDee found a blanket in the bedroom and tucked it around her, while silent tears trickled down Renee's cheeks.

"Ssh," DeeDee said, stroking her hair. "The police will take him away. You won't have to see him again." *Except at his trial*, she thought.

It was hours later and after dark when they arrived back at DeeDee's home where an ecstatic Balto greeted them by launching himself like a furry missile at the wire fence.

"I know Balto, we missed you too," DeeDee laughed, when she let him out of the fenced area of the yard. "There was quite a lot of drama today. I'm glad you were safe here at home and away from the action."

After dinner, she and Jake joined Balto on the front porch, where he played with his toy rabbit while they had a glass of wine.

"What's wrong?" Jake gave her a concerned look.

DeeDee sighed. "I guess I need to call Cassie tomorrow and tell her what's happened. I'm dreading it, because Al's certain to go ballistic. I also have a question for you. How did you just happen to have a tape recorder in your pocket?"

Jake laughed, throwing a stick across the grass for Balto to fetch. "It's lucky for Philippe he's already dead, so Al won't have to go and murder him all over again. As to your question. Every morning when I leave the house, I make sure I have my keys, my wallet, my gun, and my tape recorder. And I'd bet every other private investigator does the same. You just never know what the day's going to bring."

CHAPTER EIGHTEEN

"Close your eyes," Jake said, leading DeeDee by the hand into his house. "You have to promise not to peek, okay?"

"Um, sure," DeeDee said, feeling Balto's fur brush her legs as the dog went racing past. She reached out with her free arm, and from the feel of the furniture, knew they were in Jake's living room. The sound of the sliding doors being pulled open was a definite clue that they were about to go outside onto the patio.

"There's a step, so be careful," Jake said, confirming her suspicions. "You can sit down now," he said, pulling out a chair, and helping her into it. "Don't move, I'll be back in a minute."

DeeDee tried to open one of her eyes a tiny slit so she could find out what was going on, but Jake's voice calling from inside made her clamp it shut again. "DeeDee, I can see your eyes twitching. Don't even think about it."

"Sorry," she replied. "I forgot you have security cameras everywhere." She relaxed in the chair, and could hear Jake turn on some romantic music. Something else was odd. She sniffed. The smell of cooking reached her nostrils. It was a divine smell, not Jake's usual entree of steak or ribs, although she liked those too.

"I must be dreaming," she called out. "Is that *coq au vin* I smell?"

The sound of Jake's footsteps on the patio indicated he'd returned. She could also hear Balto panting. "What are you two up to? I'm dying to find out," DeeDee squealed.

There was a pop, and the hiss of something fizzy being poured, then Jake gave her permission to open her eyes.

DeeDee gasped in amazement. Jake's patio was decorated with hanging glass lanterns with tea lights flickering inside, the table laid like they were in a French bistro, and a silver ice bucket containing a bottle of champagne was in a stand next to the table. Balto, wearing a black bow tie for a collar, sat proudly at attention, watching the scene unfold.

Jake handed her a champagne flute from across the table, and she accepted the glass, taking a sip.

"What's going on?" she asked in bewilderment. "Are we celebrating something?"

Jake raised his glass and clinked it against hers. "Let's see," he said, raising an eyebrow. "Don't you think the fact that a whole week has passed without anyone getting murdered is celebration enough?"

"Maybe," DeeDee smiled, "but I don't think that's it."

"You'd be right," Jake said, patting his leg for Balto to come over to him. He bent down and whispered something in Balto's ear, and Balto solemnly walked over to DeeDee.

"What the…" DeeDee looked down at where Balto had dropped a small Tiffany box tied in a bow at her feet. She picked it up, and thought she might cry. "Is this…?"

Jake nodded. "Open it," he whispered.

DeeDee pulled the ribbon and opened the ring box. Twinkling back at her was a platinum two-carat emerald-cut diamond ring with trapezoid-shaped side stones in smaller diamonds.

"Do you like it?" Jake asked.

DeeDee nodded, her eyes brimming with tears.

"This might be the first time I've ever seen you speechless," Jake said, coming around to DeeDee's side of the table. He got down on one knee, and reached for DeeDee's hand. "I know my first proposal wasn't the most romantic, but it came from the heart. Now that we have our children's blessings, I thought it might be nice to do it properly. DeeDee, will you marry me?"

DeeDee nodded, and whispered "Yes," while Jake slipped the ring onto her finger. She held out her hand, admiring how the diamonds sparkled in the moonlight, and leaned over to kiss Jake softly on the lips.

A familiar face poked her head out from behind the sliding doors. "I'm glad that went well. Are you two lovebirds ready to eat?"

DeeDee burst out laughing. "Susie! No wonder I couldn't get ahold of you today. I was wondering where you'd disappeared to."

Jake stood up and went back to his seat. "You don't think I did this all by myself, do you? I know I can do a decent barbecue, but *coq au vin's* completely out of my league. I thought I'd better call in an expert to make sure nothing went wrong."

"That was a good idea." DeeDee took another sip of her champagne. "I'll send you the bill tomorrow."

When they were almost finished eating, Susie discreetly closed the sliding doors, and DeeDee knew she was cleaning up in the kitchen.

"I'll get out of your way," Susie said, when they were done and she had cleared the plates away. "Dessert's in the refrigerator. Good night."

"Thanks, Susie," DeeDee said, smiling. "Tonight was perfect." She looked across at Jake. "And thank you. Let's get married sooner rather than later."

Jake's face turned serious. "I'd like that too," he said. "But first, there's something I need to run past you."

DeeDee grew solemn too, while Jake told her what was on his mind. "A good friend of mine, Alex, who served in the Marines with me, has asked a favor of me. He's a private investigator, and he wants me to help him out in his business for a while. I wanted to talk to you about it before I gave him my answer."

"I don't see any problem with that," DeeDee said, "if that's what you want."

"It's not that simple. Alex lives on the East coast, in Connecticut. His wife is terminally ill with cancer. He has three young kids, and he wants to be there for them as well as take care of his wife. It would mean that we'd leave Bainbridge Island and go there to live. No one can say how long his wife's got. The doctors have told him it could be weeks, or maybe months."

DeeDee sat in silence while she thought about this turn of events. She looked over at Jake, his earnest face eager for her response. The answer came to her quickly, without any angst or doubt crossing her mind. "Of course we have to go," she said, knowing that Jake would never desert a friend in need. "But what about your business here on Bainbridge Island?"

Jake's face broke into smile. "I've thought about that. I think I know someone who might be able to cover for me. I haven't asked him yet, because I wanted to talk this over with you first."

DeeDee giggled. The champagne had gone to her head. "Do I know this person? Is it—"

Jake nodded.

"Al De Duco," they said in unison.

"I think he just might do it," DeeDee said. "What a genius idea."

Jake hesitated. "What about Deelish? I don't want your business to suffer as a result of this either."

"That's easy," DeeDee said. "Susie is more than capable of looking after Deelish while we're gone. I'll ask her tomorrow, but I'm sure it won't be a problem."

She raised her glass once more to Jake. "To us. I can't wait to be DeeDee Rogers."

EPILOGUE

The tinkle of a bell sounded above his head as Colin James pushed open the heavy door of the Germain Plein Air Art Gallery in Pioneer Square. It was a sunny afternoon, and after his regular visit to The Daily Grind, Colin had just been to his third session with the relationship psychologist his friend Ben had told him about, and whose office was downtown.

He looked around for a few minutes before a young woman greeted him. "May I help you, sir, or are you just browsing today?"

Colin turned to the woman and smiled. He remembered what the psychologist had said about him needing to open the lines of communication with women he met. A smile was as good an opener as any. He wasn't intending to flirt with the woman. He was just doing the homework June, his psychologist, had given him. He had to speak to a new woman every day, even if it was just to ask directions or talk about the weather.

"It's a lovely day, isn't it?" Colin said, and the woman looked at him strangely. When he'd first glanced at her, he'd thought she was plain-looking, but there was something attractive about her that he couldn't quite put his finger on. Maybe it was her green eyes, or her rosebud lips. Whatever it was, he found himself wanting more time to find out.

"Feel free to browse. Let me know if you need anything," the woman said. "I'm Renee, and I'll be in the office." She nodded towards a fabric panel at the back of the gallery.

"I'm Colin," he said, not wanting her to go. "I heard the owner of this gallery died a little while ago. I was sorry to hear that, as I've bought several pieces from him in the past. He was always very helpful."

"That's right," Renee said. "It was a terrible tragedy. I'm looking after things while the business is in transition. Mr. Germain's wife has moved to France. I'm not sure if she will be keeping the business, or selling it. At the moment, I don't think she knows herself."

"I see," Colin said, noticing that Renee had perfect ears. They were small, and flat, not sticky-out like his. "There's something I want to ask you. Do you know if fakes were ever involved in the paintings sold here?"

Renee took a deep breath and nodded her head. "I'm sorry to have to say the answer to that question is yes. When Mr. Germain was alive, that was the case. We don't know how many paintings were involved, or even which ones, but the person who was involved with Mr. Germain has been charged with criminal fraud. He's also the same person who has been charged with murdering Mr. Germain, and no doubt he will be going to prison for a very long time."

"I think I may have been sold some fakes," Colin said, watching Renee's face fall. "Is there any way to get the originals, since that's what I paid for?"

"No, I'm sorry. You should bring them in," Renee said, "and we'll get them checked for you. Mrs. Germain said she will compensate anyone who has been affected by the fraud committed by her deceased husband. She didn't know anything about it, and is upset beyond belief about the situation. We both are. I had no idea either."

"Don't worry," Colin said. "It's not your fault. I'll drop by again next week, if that's all right. Do you work every Wednesday afternoon? I have an appointment nearby on Wednesdays, so I could come back about the same time."

"Yes," Renee said with a shy smile, and Colin thought her teeth alignment was delightful. He would have to ask June about what to do next.

"Okay, good. Thanks. Bye." He turned to leave, but something made him stop in his tracks.

I like this woman, he thought, *and I don't need June's guidance on what I should do next. As a matter of fact, I think she would be happy with what I'm about to do.*

"Renee, would you like to go out for dinner with me?"

"Why yes, Colin, I would like that very much."

RECIPES

SOUPE AU PISTOU

Soup Ingredients:
1 ½ cups white beans
2 qts. water
1 large onion, chopped
6 large garlic cloves, minced
Bouquet garni: Three sprigs of fresh thyme and parsley. One bay leaf. Tie together with twine.
1 tbsp. olive oil
2 leeks, white and light green parts only, sliced
1 14 oz. can diced tomatoes
2 cups green cabbage, shredded
2 large carrots, diced
2 celery stalks, diced
1 medium sized zucchini, diced
½ lb. green beans, trimmed and broken into 1" pieces
½ cup small pasta shells
2 tsps. Herbes de Provence
Salt and pepper to taste

Pistou Ingredients:
2 garlic cloves, halved, green shoots removed
2 cups fresh basil leaves
½ cup extra virgin olive oil

½ cup freshly grated Parmesan cheese
Salt and freshly ground pepper to taste
½ cup freshly grated Parmesan cheese for garnish

Directions:
Soak the white beans in 6 cups of water for 6 hours and drain. Blanch the green beans in boiling water for five minutes and transfer to a bowl of ice water. Drain and set aside.

Place the white beans, along with 2 quarts of water, in a large soup pot and bring to a boil. Add half the onion, half the garlic, and the bouquet garni. Reduce the heat to low, cover, and simmer for 45 minutes. Heat the olive oil in a heavy skillet. Add the remaining chopped onion and a generous pinch of salt. Cook over medium heat, stirring, for five minutes. Add the leeks and the remaining garlic. Stir together for five minutes.

Add the tomatoes, along with the juice from the can, to the mixture and cook, stirring, for fifteen minutes. Stir this mixture into the soup pot. Add the remaining soup ingredients with the exception of the green beans and bring back to a low simmer. Cook, covered, for an hour. Add salt and pepper to taste.

To make the pistou, mash the remaining half of the garlic with a generous amount of salt with a mortar and pestle or with the back of a heavy spoon. (Sometimes I just chop it very fine. The addition of the salt makes this easy.) Using a food processor, grind the basil until it's the consistency of a paste. Add the garlic to the mixture and then add the olive oil 1 tablespoon at a time. Stir in the cheese. Put into a bowl.

After the soup has cooked for an hour, add the pasta and cook until al dente (Italian for firm to the bite. You don't want it mushy.) Taste for seasonings and adjust if necessary. Stir the green beans into the soup and cook for five minutes. Ladle the soup into bowls. Add a spoonful of the pistou on top of each soup serving and let your guests stir it in. Pass the Parmesan cheese for sprinkling on the soup. Enjoy!

BEST EVER TWICE-BAKED POTATOES

Ingredients:
4 medium size baking potatoes
¼ cup butter
¼ cup cream or half and half
½ cup shredded sharp cheddar cheese
4 slices bacon, cooked crisp and crumbled
1 bunch green onions – finely chop only the green parts
Salt and pepper to taste
2 tbsp. cooking oil
Aluminum foil

Directions:
Preheat the oven to 400 degrees. Heat the butter and cream together in a small saucepan over low heat. Rub the potatoes with the cooking oil, prick with a fork, and place on a baking sheet covered with aluminum foil. Bake the potatoes for about an hour or until soft when gently pressed. (Use a baking mitt, so your fingers don't get burned!) Cut the potatoes in half, lengthwise.

Carefully scoop out the pulp of each potato and place in a large bowl. Shells should be relatively free from pulp. Mash the potatoes (I really think using a hand masher is best) with the butter and cream mixture until it's the consistency you like (some people like it creamier than others). Stir in the cheese. Spoon the mixture back into the potato shells, piling high. Top with the crumbled bacon and green onions. Bake at 400 degrees for 15 minutes. Serve and enjoy!

LACINATA KALE SALAD

Ingredients:
10 – 12 leaves lacinata kale (also called Tuscan kale)
6 baby carrots
1 Japanese cucumber
1/3 cup shredded Manchego cheese

Juice from 1 lemon
½ cup toasted pine nuts (I toast then in a small frying pan for about 5 minutes. Don't let them burn. It's easy to do.)
¼ cup extra virgin olive oil

Directions:
Peel the carrots and cut off the ends. (I just run a knife along the sides of carrots. Seems a lot easier than using a kitchen paring device.) Parboil the carrots in boiling water until tender when pierced with a fork. Remove, allow to cool, and slice into ½" pieces.

Wash the kale and remove the spines from each leaf. Slice into thin pieces and add to a large salad bowl. Diagonally slice the cucumber and add to the bowl along with the carrots.

Dress the salad with the lemon juice and olive oil. Toss and add the Manchego cheese and the slivered pine nuts on top. Plate and enjoy!

NOTE: Kale is considered to be one of the healthiest things you can eat!

WARM FIGS, GOAT CHEESE, AND HONEY (APPETIZER OR SIDE DISH)

Ingredients:
16 walnut halves
1 tbsp. light brown sugar
1/8 tsp. salt
1/8 tsp. ground cinnamon
3 tbsp. goat cheese (If you prefer a milder cheese, use Mascarpone)
8 fresh figs, halved lengthwise
2 tbsp. honey
Parchment paper

Directions:
Preheat the oven to 500 degrees. Combine the walnuts, brown sugar, salt, and cinnamon in a small heavy-bottomed skillet. Cook over medium-high heat until the sugar melts and evenly coats the nuts, about five minutes. Remove from pan, making sure that the nuts are separate from each other. Cool.

Spoon a heaping ½ teaspoon of cheese onto each fig half and place on a parchment paper lined rimmed cookie sheet. Bake the figs for 4 minutes. Transfer the warm figs to a serving platter. Place a candied walnut on each fig half and drizzle honey over the figs. Serve and enjoy!

RASPBERRY BROWN SUGAR TART

Crust Ingredients:
7 tbsp. unsalted butter, melted
1/3 cup sugar
1/3 tsp. vanilla extract (Don't use imitation. Use the real stuff!)
1 cup plus 1 tbsp. flour
Pinch of salt

Filling Ingredients:
½ cup sugar
2 large eggs (I prefer jumbo.)
Pinch of salt
¼ cup flour
1 tsp. vanilla extract
½ cup butter, unsalted and diced
2 6 oz. containers of fresh raspberries
9 ½" tart pan with removable bottom
Baking rack

Directions:
Crust:
Preheat the oven to 375 degrees, positioning a rack in the center of the oven. Using a fork, mix the melted butter, sugar, and vanilla

together. Add the flour and salt. Stir until incorporated. Transfer mixture to tart pan and press dough evenly onto the sides and the bottom of the pan. Bake about 18 minutes. Dough will puff slightly. Transfer to a baking rack and cool.

Filling:
Mix the eggs, sugar, and salt in a medium size bowl. Add flour and vanilla and whisk until smooth. Cook the butter over medium heat in a small heavy saucepan until it becomes a deep nutty brown, stirring often, for about six minutes. Don't let it burn. Remove from the burner and allow to cool for five minutes. Add the butter to the sugar mixture and blend.

Arrange the raspberries close together, pointed ends up, in concentric circles, on the bottom of the cooled crust. Carefully pour the butter mixture evenly over the berries. Place the tart on a rimmed cookie sheet and bake about 40 minutes or until a wooden toothpick inserted into the center comes out clean. Cool the tart pan on a rack.

When ready to serve remove the sides of the tart pan. Cut into wedges, serve and enjoy!

NOTE: This can be made 1 day ahead. Refrigerate until about half an hour before serving.

Paperbacks & Ebooks for FREE

Go to www.dianneharman.com/freepaperback.html and get your FREE copies of Dianne's books and favorite recipes immediately by signing up for her newsletter.

Once you've signed up for her newsletter you're eligible to win three paperbacks. One lucky winner is picked every week. Hurry before the offer ends!

ABOUT THE AUTHOR

Dianne lives in Huntington Beach, California, with her husband, Tom, a former California State Senator, and her boxer dog, Kelly. Her passions are cooking, reading, and dogs, so whenever she has a little free time, you can either find her in the kitchen, playing with Kelly in the back yard, or curled up with the latest book she's reading.

Her award winning books include:

Cedar Bay Cozy Mystery Series
Kelly's Koffee Shop, Murder at Jade Cove, White Cloud Retreat, Marriage and Murder, Murder in the Pearl District, Murder in Calico Gold, Murder at the Cooking School, Murder in Cuba, Trouble at the Kennel, Murder on the East Coast, Trouble at the Animal Shelter, Murder & The Movie Star, Murdered by Wine

Cedar Bay Cozy Mystery Series - Boxed Set
Cedar Bay Cozy Mysteries 1 (Books 1 to 3)
Cedar Bay Cozy Mysteries 2 (Books 4 to 6)
Cedar Bay Cozy Mysteries 3 (Books 7 to 10)
Cedar Bay Cozy Mysteries 4 (Books 11 to 13)
Cedar Bay Super Series (Books 1 to 6)... good deal
Cedar Bay Uber Series (Books 1 to 9)... great deal

Liz Lucas Cozy Mystery Series
Murder in Cottage #6, Murder & Brandy Boy, The Death Card, Murder at The Bed & Breakfast, The Blue Butterfly, Murder at the Big T Lodge, Murder in Calistoga, Murder in San Francisco

Liz Lucas Cozy Mystery Series - Boxed Set
Liz Lucas Cozy Mysteries 1 (Books 1 to 3)
Liz Lucas Cozy Mysteries 2 (Books 4 to 6)
Liz Lucas Super Series (Books 1 to 6)… good deal

High Desert Cozy Mystery Series
Murder & The Monkey Band, Murder & The Secret Cave, Murdered by Country Music, Murder at the Polo Club, Murdered by Plastic Surgery

High Desert Cozy Mystery Series - Boxed Set
High Desert Cozy Mysteries 1 (Books 1 to 3)

Northwest Cozy Mystery Series
Murder on Bainbridge Island, Murder in Whistler, Murder in Seattle, Murder after Midnight, Murder at Le Bijou Bistro, Murder at The Gallery

Northwest Cozy Mystery Series - Boxed Set
Northwest Cozy Mysteries 1 (Books 1 to 3)

Midwest Cozy Mystery Series
Murdered by Words, Murder at the Clinic, Murdered at The Courthouse

Jack Trout Cozy Mystery Series
Murdered in Argentina

Coyote Series
Blue Coyote Motel, Coyote in Provence, Cornered Coyote

Midlife Journey Series
Alexis

Newsletter

If you would like to be notified of her latest releases please go to www.dianneharman.com and sign up for her newsletter.

Website: www.dianneharman.com,
Blog: www.dianneharman.com/blog
Email: dianne@dianneharman.com

SURPRISE!

MURDER AND MEGA MILLIONS

Sixth Book in the High Desert Cozy Mystery Series

Available for pre-order: http://getBook.at/MEGA

She picked the winning numbers. She won millions. Is that why she was murdered?

But who did it? Melissa's no-good uncle or her ex-con brother who she hasn't seen for years? Could they both be prime suspects? And what about her maid and her abusive husband-to-be? Is being known as a prominent philanthropist or antique collector a reason to commit murder? Yes, Palm Springs, California, is like a different world to most people, but is it different enough that ego justifies murder?

And are the rich really that different than you and me?

When Marty's wealthy new appraisal client is murdered, things get messy. Her husband's the lead detective on the case, and he needs her to help him solve the murder.

Can Marty's psychic sister help? How can Patron, her young boxer dog, seem to sense when she's in danger? And what about the ghost her sister sees? Could she really be the murder victim's mother?

This is Book 6 in the popular High Desert Cozy Mystery series by USA Today Bestselling Author and seven-time Amazon All-Star, Dianne Harman.

Order it now at: http://getBook.at/MEGA

Open your smartphone, point and shoot at the QR code below. You will be taken to Amazon where you can pre-order the book.

(Download the QR code app onto your smartphone from the iTunes or Google Play store in order to read the QR code below.)

Made in United States
Troutdale, OR
09/10/2024